Adrenalin was still rushing through Lyssa's body in tremors, provoked by that instant of locked eyes, that brief connection, the reflection of her own awareness in Ric's eyes.

She knew all the reasons why she should stay away from him, and they were numerous. Yet still, if the chance arose, she would not back away from kissing Ric. She would grab it—just to find out what it would be like to be kissed by him, to be held in his arms.

There. She'd made a decision. No more doubts. Just to satisfy her curiosity, she'd seize the moment. Then he'd go back to his world full of beautiful women, and she'd go back to hers. To the reality of raising a child alone. But at least she would have her memories.

Dear Reader

One of the best things about researching the location for PREGNANT: FATHER WANTED was trawling through recipe books and drooling over tempting pictures of southern Italian dishes.

One of the worst things? Gaining weight as a result of trawling through those same recipe books, drooling over those tempting pictures and then satisfying my self-induced hunger!

But, aside from the food, research for this book was particularly enjoyable. Lyssa is a travel writer, so she was on the move and I saw the Amalfi Coast through her eyes. Of course she was also falling in love, and this might have coloured her view a little. Only a little, though. Renowned for its rugged terrain, scenic beauty, picturesque towns and diversity, the Amalfi Coast is listed by UNESCO as a World Heritage Site.

I hope you enjoy visiting the Amalfi Coast, and taking an emotional journey with Lyssa and Ric.

Best wishes

Claire
www.clairebaxter.com

PREGNANT: FATHER WANTED

BY
CLAIRE BAXTER

MILLS & BOON®
Pure reading pleasure™

All the characters in this book have no existence outside the imagination of the author, and have no relation whatsoever to anyone bearing the same name or names. They are not even distantly inspired by any individual known or unknown to the author, and all the incidents are pure invention.

First published in Great Britain 2008
Harlequin Mills & Boon Limited,
Eton House, 18-24 Paradise Road, Richmond, Surrey TW9 1SR

© Claire Baxter 2008

ISBN: 978 0 263 86557 8

Set in Times Roman 13 on 15 pt
02-1208-48059

Printed and bound in Spain
by Litografia Rosés, S.A., Barcelona

BABY ON BOARD

From bump to baby and beyond...

**Whether she's expecting or they're adopting—
a special arrival is on its way!**

**Follow the tears and triumphs as these couples find
their lives blessed with the magic of parenthood...**

There's twin trouble in February
with Caroline Anderson's latest Romance:
Two Little Miracles

For my editor, Meg Sleightholme, with thanks for her belief and support—everything from picking up and reading my first manuscript to suggesting a Mediterranean location for this, my fourth book.

CHAPTER ONE

'YOU'RE going to Italy?'

Lyssa Belperio grinned as she nodded at her friend Chloe. 'So, do you mind keeping an eye on the apartment as usual?'

'Of course not. But I'm so jealous. Come inside and tell me about it. I'll make a coffee.'

'No.' Lyssa waved her palms at Chloe as she stepped into the neighbouring apartment. 'No coffee for me, remember?'

'Oh, that's right. I nearly forgot you were pregnant because you don't show. I have herbal tea. Peppermint, rosehip or chamomile?'

'Peppermint, please. You know the new travel magazine I told you about? The ultra-glossy one that I wrote that small piece for?'

'About shopping in Hong Kong. Yes, I remember.'

'Well, the editor emailed, offering me a commission. She wants a feature article written with the same *wit and humour* as the last one.' She made air quotes around the key words. She'd written the article in her natural voice and couldn't imagine writing any other way.

'That sounds good. She must have liked your work.'

Lyssa gave a modest shrug. 'I guess so. Anyway, this feature is about touring the Amalfi Coast.'

Chloe squealed. 'You lucky duck. All expenses paid?'

'Uh-huh. It's being sponsored by a tour company. They're going to provide a private driver and tour guide, and everything.'

'Blimey. Do you need someone to take photos for you? I have a camera phone.'

Laughing, Lyssa shook her head. 'Matilda said they'll buy them directly from a local photographer. No amateur shots needed.'

'Can you squeeze me into your suitcase, then? I'll be good, I promise.'

'I wish I could, but I travel lightly, remember?'

'Cheeky. I'm not that heavy. Anyway, you'll soon be much heavier than me.' Chloe dropped the teabags into the bin, then adopted a more serious tone. 'Are you sure it's all right to travel in your condition? What if something happens while you're away?'

'Nothing's going to happen,' Lyssa said firmly. 'I've been all over Asia; I'm sure I can handle Italy. And anyway, I'm only a little bit pregnant.'

'As opposed to completely pregnant?' Chloe held out the mug of herbal tea.

Pulling a face at Chloe, she took the mug and settled on one of the comfortable sofas. 'There's no problem with travelling at this early stage and, as I don't show yet, I figure there's no need for anyone to know.'

'Are you going to tell your parents before you go?'

'Oh, Chlo, they'll be so upset.' She took a moment to swallow the lump that had jumped to her throat at the mere mention of breaking the news to her parents, then sipped her tea before going on. 'You know what they're like.'

'They're protective.'

'They're incredibly old-fashioned.'

'Even so,' Chloe said gently, 'they'll have to know.'

Lyssa took another sip. 'I know, but I'd sooner wait till I get back. If I leave straight after telling them, there's no knowing what Dominic and Tony might do.'

'Excuse me? What do your brothers have to do with it?'

'I wouldn't put it past them to hunt down Steve and force him to agree to marry me.'

Chloe snorted. 'I'd like to see that. I wonder what they'd do? Would they actually hit him?'

Lyssa flapped her free hand. 'Chlo, don't be ridiculous. You don't like violence and you can't stand the sight of blood.'

'No, but I'd make an exception in Steve's case. After what he did to you, he deserves it.'

Shrugging, Lyssa acknowledged the little voice that said Chloe was right. 'Maybe. But I don't want anything to do with him again and I certainly don't want Dom and Tony involved.'

'So you wouldn't consider taking him back even if he came crawling with an apology and a proposal?'

'I think you know me better than that, Chlo.'

'I know that you've always dreamed of having the perfect family…husband, babies…'

'Yes, but…' After swallowing hard, Lyssa said, 'I wouldn't have chosen to be a single parent. I want my baby to have a father—one that is there to see him or her grow up—and I'm terrified of doing this on my own, but I have to. An absent father is better than a bad father.'

'Um, I hate to play devil's advocate here, but you don't know that Steve would be a bad father.'

'He hates children.' Lyssa's hand went to her stomach as if she could protect her baby from the truth. 'I can't believe I misjudged him so badly. I thought he only hated *other people's* children. I thought he'd want one of his own, but no, I was wrong.'

'Oh, well, you're better off without him, then.'

'Exactly.'

'It's just that…'

'What?'

'Well, it's going to be hard. I just want to be sure that you've thought this through, that you won't have any regrets later.'

'I won't. I'd rather be alone with my baby than married to a man who doesn't love us both completely and clearly doesn't want to be with us.'

Chloe looked as if she wanted to say more, but she pressed her lips together. She was a great friend and Lyssa felt a sudden rush of emotion. Chloe would support her no matter what. Even if she thought she'd made the wrong decision, she'd be there for her and she really appreciated that.

But she'd made the right decision where Steve was concerned.

'Anyway,' Chloe said after a resigned sigh, 'you might meet someone in Italy. You always used to talk about your Italian fantasy man.'

'Uh-uh. No way.' Lyssa shook her head. 'That was before.'

It was true that she'd dreamed for years of visiting Italy. She'd had this crazy notion about finding her soulmate there. But she'd grown up since then. She'd learned that true love itself was the fantasy.

'Not this trip. That's the very last thing I intend to do. I'm going to be a mother and that's the only relationship I'm interested in from now on.'

'But you might—' Chloe saw her expression and mimed zipping her lips.

Lyssa was serious. Nothing would stop her taking this commission. It was her dream job. But meeting a man over there was the furthest thing from her mind. Besides, no one would want her now she was pregnant. She shook her head at Chloe.

'I'm going there to work and at the same time, hopefully, get in touch with my Italian roots. Nothing more.'

Ricardo Rossetti stared at his uncle Alberto. 'But I'm no tour guide—'

'No, no, I know, but you know so much about the history of this region. More than Gino or myself. You would do a very good job and believe me, I would not ask if I were not desperate. Gino's accident is the worst thing that could have happened. I would take over myself but my doctor says I must not drive. I am sorry for Gino, of course, but this accident of his is very inconvenient.'

Ric leaned his elbows on the dinner table. His uncle's table, still covered in the remains of a very good meal, thanks to his aunt's superb cooking. He owed these people. They had always taken him in at a moment's notice—ever since his twelfth birthday and the death of his parents. He was still taking advantage of their generosity now in his adulthood. Whenever he needed to get away, to recharge, he came back to their home.

Wasn't it time he gave something back?

They both worked too hard. He didn't understand why they felt they had to expand their business now, when they should be winding down, and when his uncle's health had had a few setbacks. He wished Alberto would retire, or at least let him prop up the business financially—he could easily afford it and he'd happily do it.

But they'd never take his money.

His help, on the other hand, they could ask for without any loss of pride. And this wasn't much to ask really. All he had to do was drive some foreign woman around.

'The good thing, Ricardo,' his uncle said, 'is that this woman is from Australia. She will not have heard of you. That is good, no?'

Ric nodded. 'I'll do it, but I hope she's worth it.'

His uncle's face creased into a worried frown. 'No, no, Ricardo. You must treat her with respect, not like the women you associate with in Milano.'

'Don't worry. I'll be on my best behaviour.' He laughed, though it was a little disconcerting that his uncle seemed to know the type of woman he normally dated.

It made no difference what type of woman this travel writer might be. He wasn't interested in women of any type at the moment; he had more important things to think about. 'I meant, I hope her article is worth the effort. I hope it's good for business.'

'Yes, of course. I understand. You will be all right to drive? Your knee is better?'

Ric waved a dismissive hand. 'It's OK, Uncle. I won't be here too much longer.'

'You know your aunt and I are always happy to have you here.'

'I know, thank you.' Still, he wanted to get back to Milano. He wanted to get on with his life. This time out had been one forced on him by injury. He certainly wouldn't have chosen to take time off at this stage of his football career. But the club doctor and his management had advised him to have a complete break during his rehabilitation; to think about his future. Ominous words for any player, but for him they were horrifying.

Rome. It had a smell all of its own, Lyssa decided as she hugged herself in excitement. Traffic, food, coffee and a touch of something else...roasted chestnuts? The guide books hadn't mentioned it, but *she* would. She pulled out the small notebook she always carried with her and made a note to include the peculiar smell in her article.

Standing outside the hotel which, she'd read, was only a few hundred metres from the Colosseum—the *Colosseum*, for heaven's sake—she could hardly believe she was really here. In Rome.

How long had she dreamed of this moment?

Only all of her life. For as long as she could remember she'd listened to her father speak fondly of *bella Roma*, where he'd lived, worked, married and from where her parents had departed for a new life in Australia.

She'd love to drop her luggage in the hotel room and go for a walk. It was only a matter of minutes to the Circus Maximus and all sorts of sights…but she was tired.

So tired. After a twenty-two-hour flight— and that didn't include time spent waiting around in airports—she was exhausted.

Of course, pregnancy didn't help. She'd been weary before she'd even set foot on the plane. Add in the stress of everything that had happened before then, and it was no surprise she felt as limp as a week-old lettuce.

Turning, Lyssa manoeuvred her suitcase on its little wheels through the hotel entrance and across the marble floor. It was only mid-afternoon; she had time to catch a couple of hours' sleep and still see something of the city before bedtime. Plus, her driver wasn't due till mid-morning the next day, which meant she'd be able to do more sightseeing after an early breakfast and before she started the job itself.

Perfect.

For a couple of weeks she'd pretend that her real life didn't exist. It would be waiting for her when she returned and she'd have the difficult job of telling her parents about her pregnancy, but for a little while she'd forget about that.

After checking in Lyssa made her way to her room, showered, then flung herself into bed. Although she'd been born in Australia, she'd obviously absorbed so much of her father's love for this place that coming here felt like coming home. She closed her eyes and drifted towards sleep on the strangely comforting blanket of sound—Vespas, sirens and car horns—coming from the streets below.

A moment later, Lyssa woke to the ring of the telephone.

She tried to make sense of the rapid-fire Italian pouring from the phone then, puzzled, peered at the time in the digital display.

Finally, the facts fell into place. Far from having only just fallen asleep, she'd slept right through the night and well into the next day! And rather than running late as she'd expected, her driver was waiting for her outside the hotel.

She'd barely put the phone back on its hook before she'd leapt out of bed and was on her

way to the bathroom. With no time to wash her
hair, she scraped it back from her face. She'd
normally use a hair straightener to counter the
natural wave that always reappeared overnight
and made her hair unruly at best. Straight hair
made her look more sophisticated, even older,
but today a pony-tail would have to do.

Back in the bedroom she pulled jeans and a
T-shirt from her case. She'd intended to start off
the tour in a smart suit and only revert to her
standard travelling gear once they were well
away from the city. But that idea went the way
of the smart hairdo. Speed won out over style.

Ric let out an impatient sigh, checked his watch
again and leaned back against his Lamborghini
Gallardo. His uncle had wanted him to use the
minibus but he'd been adamant. It was bad
enough having to act as a tour guide without
looking the part too.

Not that there was anything wrong with the
minibus his uncle used—for a family man. But
he was not a family man and he had no intention of becoming one. Giving up his car was
beyond the limit of what he was prepared to do
for this woman.

The hotel door opened and he lifted his head

to see a young girl hesitate, look to her left, then right, and go back inside. A pretty girl, she reminded him of his sisters and he wondered how they were getting on at boarding-school. He should contact them; it had been a while.

He was still watching the entrance when the girl reappeared, this time with the concierge he'd spoken to earlier. After scanning the parked cars, the concierge pointed in Ric's direction.

Frowning, he saw the girl nod then head towards him, wheeling a large suitcase behind her.

'*Buon giorno,*' she said when she stopped in front of him. '*Mi chiamo Lyssa Belperio.*'

Ric stared at her.

This was the important visitor his uncle wanted to impress? This was the woman who was going to kick-start their push to attract Australian tourists?

Couldn't be. She was too young. He glanced over her shoulder, half expecting her mother to join them. But no, she seemed to be alone.

'Lyssa Belperio,' he repeated. 'The travel writer from Australia?' he asked in English.

'Yes, that's me.' Her broad smile made her look even younger.

'Ric Rossetti.' He held out his hand and

watched her face for any sign of recognition. As expected, there was none. Instead her eyes flickered to the car behind him.

'Um…the paperwork I was given said the tour would be in a minibus.'

'Normally, yes, but I'm afraid it's unavailable.' When she gave the car a doubtful look, he said, 'I hope that's not a problem?'

She shrugged. 'I guess not. But will there be room for my suitcase?' she asked, peering at the short rear end of the Lamborghini.

'Of course.' He took the case from her and went to the front of the car. It was a tight fit with his own bag already there, but he managed to squeeze in her case too. He returned to open the passenger door for her.

She grinned. 'The engine's at the back, I hope? It does have one?'

He smiled back, nodding. 'Oh, yes, it definitely has one.'

He'd expected someone…different. Older, sophisticated, stylish. But Lyssa Belperio… well, she was none of those things. As she settled in the low seat, he shook his head. In her pink trainers, jeans and baggy pink T-shirt she looked like one of the many backpackers that thronged the piazzas of Rome.

Once inside the car he removed the baseball cap he'd worn to avoid being recognised in the street and tossed it into the space behind the two seats. He wouldn't like to think of either of his sisters travelling overseas alone and unprotected. Sharing a car with a strange man for weeks. What were her parents thinking of?

It was lucky he would be around to make sure she was safe for the duration of her stay.

Uncle Alberto's warning had been unnecessary. Getting involved with someone like Lyssa would be completely alien to him. He dated women who knew the rules of the game, who were not expecting anything beyond a good time.

Women, not girls.

Lyssa drank in the sights as Ric manoeuvred the car out of the traffic-clogged streets of Rome. In most cities, she'd have to go to a museum to see the type of history that here people lived with every day.

Crumbling statues, fountains, ancient monuments and ornate churches. Twenty-first-century traffic passing two-thousand-year-old ruins. History, graffiti, advertising and art mixing together madly.

And then there were the beautiful people.

Sexy Roman women who all seemed to be dressed in the latest designer fashions. Not that she'd know anything about that—she wouldn't know a Valentino from a Versace and she'd skipped the section in the guide book about shopping. But she could see that they had style, these women.

She settled back as they left the city behind and took the *autostrada* south. So much for her chance to see Rome, but she couldn't complain. She was here to do a job and that was to write about this company's tours of the Amalfi Coast.

How could anyone complain about an all-expenses-paid opportunity to see one of the world's most beautiful stretches of coastline?

Besides, once she'd finished working she'd have a couple of days in Rome before catching the flight home. It was all good.

Talking of good, she sneaked a glance at her driver. No tour guide she'd ever met before had looked liked this. Leaning against the flash car in his charcoal suit—designer, she assumed—and white shirt, open at the neck, he'd looked more like a model or a movie star than a driver. Even the baseball cap couldn't spoil the image.

As she'd walked up to the car, eyes as dark as espresso coffee had studied her and she hadn't liked the fluttering that had started up in her stomach in direct response. It had seemed as if he was totally focused on her, and she'd had the oddest feeling that she knew him.

She didn't know him, of course. Although…

She sucked her bottom lip between her teeth. It was ridiculous, but he looked exactly like the fantasy man she'd imagined years ago when she'd first dreamed about travelling to Italy.

Now that he'd lost the cap she could see his dark hair, short but just long enough to curl, and, combined with the sharp line of his jaw and straight nose, the look caused a quiver of recognition in her stomach.

She turned to stare out of the window without seeing the cars that whizzed by. It was weird that she remembered her fantasy with such clarity. She'd been with Steve for a couple of years, and there had been boyfriends before him. But talking about the dream with Chloe had probably kept the image alive over the years.

She jumped as a car horn blasted right next to her window.

'OK?'

She nodded at Ric, who was expertly darting in and out of lanes of traffic. Convinced now that Italian drivers were obsessed with testing the decibel count of their car horns, she was glad the tour company had insisted on collecting her from Rome. If she'd had to drive south alone, she'd have been a nervous wreck.

'Where are we heading?'

'Salerno. We'll eat lunch there.'

'Lunch? How long will it take us to get there?'

'Three, maybe three and a half hours.'

'Oh, boy. That long?' But she was hungry now. That was one thing she'd noticed about being pregnant—the outrageous hunger. Well, that and the tiredness. At least she'd escaped morning sickness. So far, anyway.

'Do you think we could stop somewhere to eat before then? Soon? I didn't have time for breakfast and I'm…' She stopped. There was absolutely no need for him to know about her condition. 'I'm hungry,' she finished hurriedly.

He shot her a glance. 'You should have said. I'll find a *pasticceria*, yes?'

'Yes.' Oh, yes. That sounded good.

Within minutes, Ric had turned off the *auto-strada* and Lyssa had time to look at the scenery, the creamy-coloured cows and clusters of terra-cotta-roofed houses clinging to the sides of hills.

He drove into a small town and parked at the

end of a higgledy-piggledy line of cars that made Lyssa smile. It was just so…Italian. There was no other word for it.

CHAPTER TWO

Lyssa stood in front of the sparkling glass cabinets, pondering her choice with as much awe as if she'd been staring at a Michelangelo sculpture or a fresco by Raphael.

The cases were crammed with artistically arranged trays of focaccias, filled panini and bowls of brightly coloured fruit. Finally she settled on a panini piled high with ham, salami, mortadella, fontina and pecorino.

They carried their purchases outside to a tiny table in the shade of a striped awning. After a few mouthfuls, Lyssa sat back with a contented sigh.

'Better?' Ric asked.

'Much. I'm sorry about the delay. I know you probably have a timetable to keep to.'

'No, not at all. The philosophy of Amalfitori is to be flexible, to fit in with whatever the clients want to do, to create a unique and unforgettable holiday experience for them.

'Nothing about the tours is "off-the-shelf". We aim to satisfy our clients' individual wishes while ensuring total immersion in the life and culture of the area.'

She chuckled. 'That sounded like a well-practised sales spiel.'

Ric broke into a grin that made his eyes sparkle. One cheek dimpled and Lyssa suppressed another sigh. He really was exceptionally good-looking and if this trip had taken place at another time, in another life…

But there was no point in letting herself think that way. No point at all.

'I practised it specially for you,' he said with a wry smile, 'for the important travel writer I had to make an effort to impress, but you don't seem very impressed.'

She shrugged. 'I've heard so many of those speeches and read so many brochures, they all sound the same after a while.'

'So what does impress you about the places you visit, then? It's important that I know. I need to make sure you don't leave disappointed.'

'It's hard to say.' She picked at a piece of ham that was falling from the panini. 'Often it's the smallest things. You know, if the waiters in a town are unfriendly, or a hotel's receptionist is helpful—it all influences your opinion. But then, it's important to remember that other travellers might have a very different experience, so you have to try to remain objective when you write the story.'

He nodded.

'Of course, bigger things can make a difference too. If, say, you visit a town where there's a vibrant festival going on and the whole place is buzzing with excitement, and the next day you visit another where the streets are empty and everyone seems to be asleep, you're going to gain very different impressions of the two towns. But on another day, it might be reversed. You see what I mean?'

'How long have you been doing this for a living?'

'Five years, give or take.'

'No. You don't look…'

'Old enough? I know. I'm twenty-six but I look about eighteen, don't I?'

'Well—'

'No, don't bother.' She flapped a hand. 'There's no correct answer. Actually, I do look older when I've had time to prepare…

clothes, make-up. But you took me by surprise this morning.'

'I'm sorry.'

'No, don't apologise. It's good that you were on time. Makes a good impression.'

Smiling again, he said, 'Well, that's a start. I did something right.'

Lyssa nodded, her mouth full, and Ric waited till she'd finished chewing before he spoke again.

'Do you enjoy being a travel writer?'

'I *love* it. It's the best job in the world.'

'And have you been to Italy before?'

'No. Actually this is the first time I've been to Europe. Until now all of my jobs have been nearer to home—Asia, New Zealand, the Pacific islands.'

He frowned, a vertical line appearing between his eyebrows. 'Are you saying you travelled through Asia on your own?'

'Oh, yes; Asia is—'

'But anything could have happened to you.'

Indignant, she pulled herself up straighter. 'I'm tougher than I look. I'm perfectly capable. I can cope with any unforeseen incidents.'

He held up his palms in apology. 'I interrupted you. Please, go on.'

She studied his face for a moment before,

deciding he was genuinely apologetic, she continued. 'As I was saying, Asia is fantastic, of course, but I've been looking forward to Europe for so long. Italy especially, since my family is Italian. I'm fascinated by the history you have all around you here.'

'Asia has history.'

'Oh, it does, of course, but it's different. I love to hear about the Romans, Greeks, Carthaginians, Trojans.'

'Ah, well, I can give you what you want. You should leave here a very happy woman.'

'I'm sure I will.' She didn't flatter herself that there was a double meaning to his words, but even so, warmth in the region of her throat felt suspiciously like the start of a blush. She quickly bent her head to examine the panini.

'Would you like a coffee before we set off again?'

She'd *love* one. A hefty dose of caffeine would go down very nicely right now, but since the positive test result she'd been revolted by the taste. She fervently hoped this was one side effect that would be reversed as soon as the baby was born.

She shook her head. 'Just water for me, thanks.'

Moments later Ric placed a glass of iced

water in front of her and a frothy cappuccino on his side of the table.

She wasn't turned off by the strong aroma of coffee, just the taste. She inhaled deeply then took a gulp of water and watched enviously as he scooped up froth. 'I thought no self-respecting Italian would drink cappuccino after breakfast?'

'It's still early enough to count as breakfast time,' he said in a serious tone.

'Right.'

'I'd like to think I am a self-respecting Italian.'

She winced. She really should think before she spoke. 'No offence intended.'

A smile tugged at his lips and she saw the teasing light in his eyes. 'None taken. Did you know the cappuccino was invented by Capuchin monks?'

'No, I didn't.'

'They used coffee to keep them awake through the long nights of religious practice.'

'And millions of people are grateful to them.'

She caught her breath at the sparkle in Ric's eyes as he lifted his cup. It was a good thing she didn't have the slightest interest in him as a man, because he certainly had a lot to be interested in. Just the way his eyes glinted could almost make her forget she was nearly a mother.

He'd left the dark suit jacket back in the car and the crisp white shirt showed off his broad shoulders and slim waist. And then, she thought with a silent sigh, there was the way he moved. Without being obvious, she'd watched him go inside earlier and really, he was wasted as a tour guide. With his height and his lean shape he was more suited to…well, anything.

Actually, she suspected he must have a lucrative second source of income to own the type of car he drove. Either that, or being a tour guide paid much more than writing about those same tours.

Not that it was any of her business.

Looks weren't everything, she reminded herself. Ric Rossetti might turn out to be a bore at best, and she had to spend three weeks with him.

By the time they'd arrived in Salerno and Ric had pointed out some of the historical sites, Lyssa was starving again. They wandered along the main boulevard, Corso Umberto, and she was relieved when Ric led her down a tiny street to a little restaurant. She hoped the portions weren't on the small side too.

The owner came forward to greet Ric and

was clearly pleased to see him. They'd barely settled at their table before they were served a beautifully displayed platter of antipasto.

'Unless you'd prefer to order from the menu, Roberto would like to surprise us.'

'Ooh, yes. Let him surprise us. As long as it's food and plenty of it, I'll be happy.'

Ric laughed. 'You can rest assured on that score.'

'The owners are friends of yours?'

'Not exactly. I'll order a bottle of frascati, shall I?'

'Not for me, thanks.' She pointed at the thick green jug on the table. 'I'll stick to water.'

'Are you sure? Would you prefer something else? Lambrusco, or Prosecco?'

'No, thanks. I don't drink at all, but don't let that stop you ordering whatever you want.'

He shook his head at the hovering waiter and poured them both water from the frosty jug.

Surprised, she asked him about Salerno while they ate antipasto and was soon astonished by the level of detail he was able to provide about any period of history—from the Goth to the Norman occupations of the town—and yet she was far from bored.

He paused while she got excited over the

arrival of ravioli filled with crabmeat in a buttery sauce. She sniffed at the bowl before taking a forkful of the creamy pasta. She closed her eyes for just a moment, then opened them to see Ric watching her with that sparkle of amusement in his eyes again.

He smiled. 'The plan was to see some more of the town this afternoon, then stay overnight and set out from here on the Amalfi Coast drive tomorrow. But, since you like history, perhaps you'd prefer to head south this afternoon, to visit Paestum?'

'I've never heard of Paestum.'

'It was an ancient Greek city which was abandoned in the ninth century AD, mainly because of malaria, since it was surrounded by marshes. It gradually became buried by swamps and it was forgotten about for nine hundred years until the construction of a new road, when it was rediscovered and excavated. They found three well-preserved temples as well as other buildings.'

'Oh, wow, that sounds great. I'd love to visit if we can fit it in.'

'No problem. I'll make a call and arrange a hotel down there for tonight.'

Lyssa grinned at the waiter as he placed grilled

sea bream with a salsa verde and fried artichokes in front of her. 'This looks wonderful.'

Then, as she was about to start eating, a man with the deepest wrinkles she'd ever seen approached their table.

'*Scusi, mi scusi.*'

He smiled at Ric and spoke in a stream of Italian that Lyssa had no hope of following. He didn't seem to care, he had eyes only for Ric, so she settled back to enjoy the meal.

Moments later the man pulled a piece of paper from his pocket, borrowed a pen from a passing waiter and thrust them both at Ric, who, she thought, was very patient with the old man as he scribbled on the paper and smiled at the man's profuse thanks.

Puzzled, she watched the man walk away then asked, 'Did you just give him your autograph?'

He nodded and picked up his cutlery. 'How's your food?'

'Brilliant. Look, I know I'm being nosy, but I'm intrigued to know what that was all about.'

'How much did you understand?'

'Hardly anything. I wasn't listening, actually. I was eating.'

'Good choice. Roberto's chef is one of the best in my opinion.'

'So...?'

For a moment she thought he wasn't going to explain, but then he looked up and his dark eyes locked with hers.

'I should explain. I play football. For one of Italy's major clubs. In Milano.'

'Oh.' She nodded. 'That explains the car.'

He smiled. 'Yes. I refused to use the minibus.'

She tilted her head. 'My brothers are sport mad. They watch the Italian soccer—that's what we call football back home—on the sports channel.'

'Do they?'

'Yes. They might even have heard of you.'

She didn't like football herself. She didn't think much of the players either. From what she knew of sportsmen—at least, those who made the news—most of them seemed to be insensitive, looks-obsessed jerks. She didn't like their hedonistic lifestyles, nor the way they treated their wives and girlfriends.

Knowing Ric was part of that world put things into perspective for her. He might be extraordinarily good-looking, but he was not her type at all. And she clearly wasn't his type either, since she wasn't a blonde bimbo.

The thought of bringing up her baby in that

world repulsed her, which was fine, as there was not the remotest chance of that happening.

'I don't get it myself.' She shrugged. 'I don't understand why people become so passionate about it. It's just a game.'

'We'll have to agree to disagree, then.'

'Yes.' She narrowed her eyes and looked at him thoughtfully. 'Another thing I don't understand is why you're working as a tour guide. You can't possibly need the money.'

After a short burst of laughter, he said, 'No, I don't. You're very direct, aren't you?'

'Direct is a nice way of putting it. I speak without thinking most of the time. It's a bad habit. I really should try to fix it.'

'No, I like it.'

Her eyes met his and she felt a jolt as her insides reacted to his words. *Pathetic*, she told herself. She wasn't so starved of affection that she could be affected by a statement that wasn't even a real compliment.

Or was she?

She cleared her throat. 'So, the tour guide thing?'

'It is my uncle's business. I've been staying with my uncle and aunt. Their regular driver, Gino, had an accident. It wasn't his fault but he has a broken leg and he was supposed to drive you, so they asked me to help out.'

'I see.'

She smiled and nodded at Roberto when he appeared at their table to check they were enjoying their meal, then returned her gaze to Ric, curious to know more.

'Shouldn't you be in Milan now?'

'No.' Something flashed in his eyes but it had gone before she'd had time to work out what it was. 'I'm on rehabilitation leave. I've had a knee reconstruction.'

'Oh, I'm sorry. That must be so frustrating.'

'It is.' He took a drink of water, then sighed. 'And it's not my first operation on the same knee. I've been through the whole recovery period before.'

She clicked her tongue in sympathy. 'Aren't you worried about being recognised?'

Ric flicked a dismissive wave. 'I might be recognised, but it shouldn't be a problem. Not here. In Milan, yes, it can be a nuisance. In other cities, Rome for instance, possibly. But generally I find the paparazzi limit themselves to covering high-profile events or the celebrity nightspots. My day-to-day activities aren't normally interesting enough for the media, and down here I don't think we'll see any photographers.'

'What about fans?'

'They're rarely a problem. Like the man who came to the table today, they're usually polite. They deserve to be treated politely in return. These people spend their hard-earned money to go to games. The least they deserve is respect. I hope you don't object if we have the occasional interruption?'

'No, not at all.'

After thanking Roberto for the delicious food and refusing a *gelato* to follow—even she had finally eaten enough—they got up from the table. As they headed for the door she wondered whether Ric had a girlfriend and, if he did, whether she matched the image Lyssa had of footballers' women. Supermodel-slim. Perfectly groomed. Tall. All the things she wasn't.

She didn't have body issues, but she was just an average woman and fully aware of her shortcomings. These sports people lived like rock stars and they had the women to match. She'd thought of them as *bimbos*, but that might be unfair. She shouldn't judge them for choosing to obsess about their looks.

She wasn't interested in Ric, so it made no

difference, but still she felt a little spear of disappointment that she could never have been his type even if things had been different for her.

She shook off the feeling as they emerged into the bright spring sunshine and Ric excused himself to make a phone call. She was being silly. She was here to do a job and she had no business being attracted to Ric. The fact that he was completely out of her league was just an additional reason not to entertain such a ridiculous notion.

Later, Lyssa gazed at the majestic Poseidon Temple with the Basilica standing next to it in a field of wild red poppies. She listened to Ric explaining that it was built around the same time as the Parthenon in Athens and was considered the best preserved example of a Doric temple in the world.

It wasn't the accent that made his speech so entertaining, and it wasn't the facts, though he had a way of including details that fascinated her. No, there was something about his smooth-as-velvet voice combined with his matter-of-fact manner that made her want to listen to every word.

'Since you're not a real tour guide, how do

you know so much about the history of the place?' she asked as they turned to head back to the car.

He shrugged. 'What can I say? Even as a child, I found it interesting.'

'Did you grow up around here?'

'Yes.'

'Do your parents still live here?'

'They died the day I turned twelve.'

She sucked in a breath through her teeth. 'Both at once?'

'Yes. Car accident.'

'I'm so sorry,' she said, her heart going out to him. She hesitated, but was unable to resist asking, 'Who did you live with after the accident?'

'I moved in with my uncle and aunt.'

'The ones who own Amalfitori?'

'Yes.'

They were strolling slowly and he was a step ahead of her, making it difficult to see his face, but his voice sounded as matter-of-fact as ever, as if he didn't find the subject painful.

Or maybe he was just good at hiding it.

'Were you an only child?'

'No, my sisters were babies. My uncle and aunt took them in too. They required a lot of attention.'

'Did they have children of their own as well?'

'Yes. Older children. My cousins were sixteen, seventeen and nineteen.'

Too old to be interested in the same things as a twelve-year-old, she assumed. Not an only child, then, but probably a lonely one.

He turned to gesture to her to go ahead of him and she saw the sadness in his eyes. She had to swallow before speaking again. 'So you had to find something to occupy yourself and history was it?'

For a moment he looked surprised, as if he hadn't expected her to understand, but then he nodded. 'You're right. I spent hours studying history books.'

After a pause, she said, 'Well, thanks for the suggestion, Paestum was definitely worth the visit.'

'You're welcome. It's in my interests to make you happy.' His dimple appeared as he smiled. 'And you're easy to please.'

His protective hand on her back as he guided her past a group of tourists was pleasing her at that moment. She told herself not to be quite so easily pleased. She couldn't afford to be an idiot.

'Well…' she walked away from his hand, moving to her side of the car and looking at him across the roof '…I hope you can keep up the high standard you've set.'

'I intend to.'

After he'd steered the car back onto the road, he said, 'You mentioned you had brothers.'

'Mmm. Older brothers. Two.'

'Did they look after you when you were growing up?'

She blew out a breath. 'If, by that, you mean did they frighten off every boy who came near me, yes, they did.'

He chuckled. 'Good. That's what brothers are supposed to do.'

Groaning, she said, 'They were so annoying. When I went out with a group of friends, they'd turn up to keep an eye on me. You don't do that to your sisters, do you?'

'No,' he said with a grimace, 'but only because they're away at school in Switzerland.'

'Boarding-school?'

'Yes. Well, I thought it was the best option under the circumstances. My uncle and aunt shouldn't have the responsibility, and they're not easy girls to keep under control.'

'Do you see them at all?'

'Of course. Whenever I can. I haven't abandoned them if that's what you're thinking.'

She searched his face. Satisfied by what she saw, she relaxed. 'Well, I found out much later that my brothers had ulterior motives. It wasn't only me they were keeping an eye on, it was my friends.'

She rolled her eyes.

'Oh.'

'Yes, *oh*. It was all right for them to go out with girls of my age, but not for me to go out with boys of their age. Or of any age for that matter.'

'What about your parents? What did they think?'

'Oh, they were no help at all. They were so strict. They didn't like me mixing with Australian girls because they thought they'd corrupt me. If they could have done they'd have locked me away till I was married, though how I'd have met anyone to marry I don't know.'

She heaved a sigh from deep inside. 'Honestly, growing up in an Italian family in a country like Australia was difficult at times.'

'Difficult? How?'

'Don't get me wrong, I've had a fabulous life and I'm grateful, but it's the whole caught-between-two-cultures thing. My parents were stuck in the old ways, the ways they grew up with, but I was part of a different world. I'm sure things had changed where they'd come from too, but they couldn't believe that because they couldn't see it with their own eyes. You know what I mean?'

'I can see how that would be a problem.'

'Everything I wanted to do was different from the way things were done in their youth, therefore it was wrong. Clothes, music, dancing…and they blamed the new country for all of it.'

He shot her a glance. 'So you weren't allowed to be like your friends?'

'No. Oh, and my *nonna* lived with us too. She was so embarrassing.'

'Embarrassing how?'

'Well, I'd be at school lining up at the canteen to buy lunch like everyone else—a burger or a meat pie or something—when my *nonna* would turn up with this enormous meal she'd cooked for me. She expected me to sit down and eat it while she watched, and she was very hard to refuse.'

She waved away Ric's laughter. 'You might think it's funny, but I can tell you, it wasn't at the time. Then there was shopping. Oh, my goodness, you have no idea what that was like.'

'Why?'

'Well, fruit and vegetables, for example. I don't know what it's like here, but over there the shopkeepers don't like you to touch them. They put up signs to that effect. But both my mother and my *nonna* just pretended they couldn't read English and went ahead and poked and prodded everything in the shop. They practically squeezed all the juice out of something before they decided it wasn't good enough to buy.'

Ric grinned. 'You're exaggerating, surely?'

'No, I am not.' Actually, she was a little, but it had been good to hear Ric laugh after the sadness of their earlier conversation. 'Oh, I could go on, but I won't. Just consider yourself lucky not to have grown up overseas.'

'I will.'

'Have you travelled at all?'

'I have. I've even lived abroad. In England. I played football over there for a while.'

'Really? That explains your very good English. Did you like it there?'

'Yes, I would have liked to stay longer but…' He shrugged. 'I was on loan and my club wanted me back. Anyway, I've travelled throughout Europe and to America, but I've never been to Australia.' He turned off the main road. 'Here's the hotel.'

Lyssa sat forward as they drove through a shady pine wood. 'This is nice.'

The hotel itself was a three-storey white building, well away from the road, with arched windows opening onto wrought-iron balconies.

The beautiful young woman behind the reception desk greeted Ric with a smile. 'We've been expecting you,' she said.

Lyssa made a point of smiling at her, just to check whether she was invisible. She might as well have been for all the notice the receptionist took of her. With a resigned shrug she turned away to look around the small, elegant hotel with its ceramic-tiled floors and thick white walls. Who could blame the girl for ogling Ric? She'd had to stop herself doing the same thing—and she wasn't interested in him as a man, only as a tour guide.

Ric joined her and they made arrangements to meet later for dinner before heading off to their respective rooms.

Lyssa's high-ceilinged room had a bright blue bedspread, tubs of red pelargoniums on the balcony and a view through the pine trees to the sea. With a satisfied sigh, she sat on the edge of the bed.

It had been a busy first day and her energy level was waning. She was tempted to lie down for a while, but she'd learned her lesson. There was no such thing as a brief doze now that she was pregnant. Once her head hit the pillow she'd be out for the count.

It would make more sense to jump straight into the shower and take her time freshening up before dinner. That would definitely make her feel better.

She'd packed a few simple non-crushable dresses, her standard wardrobe for evening wear while travelling, so she pulled one out of the suitcase and took it into the bathroom with her.

After the shower, she took the time to straighten all the kinks out of her hair, then applied the make-up she hadn't had time for that morning. Finally, she slipped the simple leaf-green dress over her head and stood in front of the mirror as the slinky fabric slithered over her hips.

Not bad. She'd already gained a little weight. Not enough for anyone to guess she was pregnant—and to be honest, it was probably due more to her hefty appetite than anything else. The dress wasn't tight, but it did accentuate her curves.

She shrugged as she stepped into her only pair of high heels. It wasn't as if she was trying to impress Ric, but she did feel an irrational need to show him she could look her age—and she knew she did tonight.

The look on Ric's face as she walked into the restaurant told her he *was* impressed, and she felt a thrill despite her denial.

He was silent as he pulled out a chair for her and she caught his eye. 'How old do I look now?'

He gave her a lopsided, one-dimpled smile. 'Ancient.'

With a laugh, she took a sip of the iced water that was waiting for her on the table. 'I'll take that as a compliment.'

He nodded slowly as he sat down, and his eyes glittered as they drifted over her again.

Suddenly unsettled by his slow appraisal, she changed the subject and kept the conversation light while she ate the best potato gnocchi she'd ever tasted, then salad, cheeses and a simple *gelato* for dessert.

By the time she parted from Ric and made her way to her room, she was relaxed and happy. Certainly more relaxed and happier than she'd been for a long time.

Since she'd shared the news of her pregnancy with Steve.

Since she'd learned that at the time she needed him most, he wanted nothing to do with her.

She firmly pushed thoughts of Steve out of her mind. He was history. He had no part in her life now and she refused to waste precious time thinking about him.

She didn't want to think about how she was going to manage on her own either. For now, it was almost as if she'd entered an alternate reality, one where she didn't have to worry about the future, where she didn't have to look any further forward than the next day.

CHAPTER THREE

REMEMBERING how Lyssa had enjoyed her food the day before, Ric ordered breakfast for both of them, a feast of fruit, yoghurt, cheese, ham, bread rolls and sweet cakes. Then he sat back with his espresso to wait for Lyssa to come downstairs, surprised at how much he was looking forward to seeing her again.

It wasn't that he was attracted to her—although he had to admit he'd almost been knocked off his feet when she'd walked into the restaurant for dinner in her sexy dress—it was because she was fun to be with, and he couldn't remember the last time he'd had such simple, innocent fun with a female, the last time he'd teased, laughed and shared a joke with a woman. If ever.

She'd made him realise how rusty he was at having a platonic relationship. Almost all his relationships with the opposite sex involved just that—sex. But Lyssa didn't want any more from him than what he had to offer right now: his knowledge, protection and company—actually, she probably didn't want his protection, but she would have it whether she wanted it or not.

And she wasn't like the women he was used to. Not cynical, jaded or bored with life. There was a freshness about her that appealed to him. It did him good just to be around her positive energy.

He'd been having a miserable time lately. It was true that he was recovering from a knee operation as he'd told Lyssa, but it was more than that—he had a decision to make. One that would affect his future, his whole life. Spending time with Lyssa had already made him forget his problems for one day, and he liked the idea of forgetting them for a while longer.

Doing this favour for his uncle could be just what he needed to take his mind off his problems. They'd still be there when it was finished, but at least he'd have a brief respite from thinking about them.

Just then Lyssa entered the room and he forgot about everything as he put down his cup to stand and meet her. She was again wearing her jeans and trainers and another baggy pink

T-shirt that made her look like a teenager and hid the very grown-up curves he knew were underneath.

He thrust away the image of her in the clingy dress that had shown off just how womanly she was. He didn't want to feel a physical attraction for her. She wasn't his type and he didn't need her to be. It was enough that he found her interesting and enjoyed her company.

'Good morning. Did you sleep well?'

She beamed a smile at him. 'Like the proverbial log.' Then as she dropped her gaze to the table, her eyes lit up. 'Wow, this looks great.'

'We can't have you starting the day without breakfast again, can we?'

'No, I completely agree.'

As they ate, they discussed Ric's proposed itinerary—a leisurely drive along the coast, visiting Palinuro, Maratea and other places along the way, and arriving in Vietri sul Mare in time for lunch.

'Sounds perfect,' Lyssa said as she polished off the last of the cakes, 'and not just because you mentioned lunch.'

Ric laughed, watching her brush cake crumbs from her clothes. He couldn't remember the last time he'd had breakfast with a woman that didn't consist of coffee, gossip and not much else. Lyssa was like a breath of fresh air. 'Well, if you've finished here, we'll make a start, shall we?'

'Sure.'

The same receptionist was on duty as they checked out and Lyssa was tempted to tell the girl she was making a fool of herself smiling flirtatiously at Ric. But she kept quiet. It was none of her business and, for all she knew, Ric might plan to visit the hotel at a later date to take advantage of what the girl was clearly offering.

But he hardly seemed to notice the attention he was receiving and definitely wasn't flirting in return. Which was surprising, given the girl's exotic looks and obvious interest.

Settling back in the Lamborghini, Lyssa pulled a notepad and pen from her handbag to make notes on the trip so far. She'd deliberately left her laptop at home, not wanting to be distracted from the details of the trip by emails and so on.

This was the way she preferred to work, keeping copious notes as she went and typing them all up when she got home. It helped her to get her feelings down on paper—they seemed to flow from her fingers through her pen onto the page. Later she'd spend time finding the right words to convey those feelings to her readers. It might seem old-fashioned to some but it was her process and she had no intention of changing it.

Ric glanced across as he drove away from the hotel. 'What's the verdict? Are you going to write a favourable article?'

She chuckled. 'You'll have to wait and see. It's far too early to say—you might blot your copybook yet.'

In truth, she was a great believer in early impressions and she couldn't really imagine Ric doing anything to spoil the very favourable impression she'd gained so far. But who knew?

She slid a surreptitious glance at him. He'd forgone the suit today in favour of faded jeans and a dark blue polo shirt—probably a designer label but she wouldn't know the difference. All she knew was that he looked incredible.

She'd hoped, she'd *really* hoped that the flare of attraction she'd felt the day before would have dissipated overnight, and that the flutters she'd felt were just shock at his resemblance to the man of her dreams. But on the contrary she felt an intense awareness of his masculinity, of his muscular footballer's legs working the pedals, his strong arms on the steering wheel.

And it was so annoying. It was not what she wanted to feel at all.

With deliberate movements, she dropped the pad and pen into her bag and asked Ric about the region they were driving through. By the time they arrived in Vietri sul Mare, renowned for its many ceramic factories and shops specialising in colourful creations of clay, she felt quite the expert.

They strolled through the quaint little town, which was decorated with wall mosaics; the townspeople had even tiled the dome of their cathedral with majolica, the decorative pottery that had been of prime importance to the economy since medieval times.

Not normally one for shopping, Lyssa found herself entranced by the beautiful designs and couldn't resist buying a large, colourful platter from one of the many shops selling such items.

'I don't know how I'm going to carry this home,' she said with a rueful smile as she stepped out onto the street.

'Don't worry, we'll get it shipped.' Ric took the awkwardly shaped parcel from her. 'If you give me your address in Australia, I'll arrange it. Will it suit your home?'

Her home. She thought of the small inner-city apartment she'd shared with Steve. She wasn't even sure she'd be able to continue to pay the rent now that he'd gone, especially with her income looking uncertain. Travel writer was hardly a suitable occupation for a woman with a baby in tow, was it?

With a jerky movement, she shook off the gloomy mood that had threatened to descend for a moment. It was such a happy, colourful day, she didn't want to let any depressing thoughts intrude.

One way or another, she would earn a living, enough to pay for everything her child needed, even if she had to write nappy-rash articles for parenting magazines. Actually, that wasn't such a bad idea. She *could* write about parenting, especially the joys and challenges of being a single parent.

There were other possibilities too but she'd explore them later. In the meantime, she was here in this wonderful place. With Ric, who was still waiting for her to answer his question.

'I'll make it suit my home, even if I have to redecorate. I love it.'

Grinning, he said, 'Well, I'd say it suits you. It's bright and cheerful.'

'Oh.' She felt a glow in her cheeks and a

matching warmth in her stomach. 'I think that's the nicest thing anyone's ever said to me.'

He looked surprised. His dark eyes narrowed and focused on her. They seemed to peer right inside her, as if he could see what kind of relationship she'd had with Steve. She didn't want him seeing so much and dragged her eyes away.

'Now, where's that lunch you promised me?'

He tapped the edge of the platter. 'I'll take this back to the car before we find somewhere to eat.'

She watched him walk off with his easy, athletic stride and let out a deep sigh. He was far too attractive for her peace of mind. She had to get herself under control. He'd made one simple comment and she'd gone all gooey. *Bright and cheerful*. It was hardly an extravagant compliment. Nothing to get excited about.

Anyway, she was pregnant. She couldn't afford the luxury of getting excited about anything he said. He was off limits as anything but a tour guide.

After lunch they set off for their hotel along the two-lane road squeezed between rocky slopes on one side and, on the other, dramatic cliffs overlooking the sea hundreds of feet below.

'So, this is the famous Amalfi Coast drive?' Lyssa said between gasps of horror as they rounded a series of tight hairpin bends.

'Yes, this is it. Stunning view, isn't it?'

'Is it?' She was too terrified to take her eyes off the road—not that she was driving. A horn's blast signalled yet another bus coming around the bend towards them. 'Good grief!' she moaned. 'How much more?'

Ric shot her an amused glance. 'I thought you were an intrepid traveller?'

'Don't look at me!' she snapped. Then in a softer tone, 'Sorry about that, but please keep your eyes on the road.'

One hand clinging to the car seat, she pressed the other against her belly. The spectacular view she'd been trying not to see was doing things to her insides and she could feel her lunch churning in her stomach.

'You're really worried, aren't you?'

'I don't feel well.' She'd ask him to turn around and go back, but she knew it was out of the question on this ridiculous road. 'Will it take much longer?'

'Not too long and I won't let anything happen to you, Lyssa. I'm a good driver.'

'I know.' She groaned as the sports car rounded

the tight bends smoothly, with no screeching tyres. 'It's not your driving; it's the road.'

He took one hand from the wheel and patted her hand where it was clutching the seat. 'Don't be scared. I'll look after you.'

Relieved to see his hand return to the wheel, she closed her eyes. The momentary contact had been comforting, but it couldn't alter the fact that she felt nauseous.

'It's worse in peak season,' he said, 'when the road is full of foreign bus drivers.'

A good reason to be glad she'd travelled early in May, Lyssa thought. After what seemed like hours, Ric turned off the road, drove through a terraced orchard and stopped in front of a low white building. Their hotel.

'You look very pale,' he said as she stepped out of the car.

She felt the blood draining from her face even as he spoke. With one hand on her back and one under her elbow, he assisted her into the reception area and she was grateful for the support.

She sat in a chair while Ric checked in, then he escorted her to her room.

'You should probably lie down for a while,' he said and she could see the genuine concern in his face.

She wanted to thank him for his help but instead she nodded and went inside, too ill to speak. She'd never known nausea like this.

Yes, the drive had been scary, but it was more than that. Maybe it was hormones. Maybe morning sickness had finally caught up with her, a bit late in the day. But what a time for it to happen.

Shutting herself in the bathroom, she gave in to the inevitable and afterwards was glad to flop onto the bed and let sleep overwhelm her.

Later, showered and changed and feeling one hundred per cent better, Lyssa found Ric sitting out on the large terrace, which he had all to himself. His worried expression as he stood and came towards her made her smile.

'I'm fine, I'm fine,' she said before he'd asked the question. 'Hey, this is lovely.' She moved to the low stone wall of the terrace, which seemed to be suspended in mid-air above the coastline.

She gazed out over a great swathe of hot-pink bougainvillea. She was a travel writer; she earned her living describing fantastic views, but this one left her lost for words.

Even the colour of the sea defeated her.

Azure, turquoise, sapphire…nothing was quite right. It lay like a sheet of glittering glass, not ruffled by even a breath of wind.

Aquamarine, she decided, then tilted her head. No, it was indescribable.

At the horizon it blended into the cloud-free sky. Below her the coastline was indented by bays and inlets, and here and there she could see pastel-coloured buildings that seemed to be tumbling down the cliffs amidst the lush vegetation.

To her right a cluster of tightly packed white houses rose up the hillside, dominated by a cathedral's dome. 'Amalfi?'

Ric had joined her at the wall. 'Yes.'

She spread her hands out wide. 'It's hard to believe it's all real,' she said in a subdued voice.

'I know what you mean. It's awe-inspiring.' After a moment's silence, he said, 'I was thinking, we could stay here for a few days, use the hotel as a base for trips when you feel well enough, and the rest of the time just relax. There's a swimming pool.' He waved a hand towards the side of the building. 'What do you think?'

What she thought was that she was perfectly well…but the idea of resting here for a while in this paradise did appeal. In fact, she didn't know how she'd be able to tear herself away.

'I like it.' She broke into a smile as she turned to face him. 'I like everything so far.'

He smiled back. 'I'm glad to hear it.' His dark eyes held hers for a long moment, and she felt her bones start to melt.

No! This wasn't what she wanted. She dragged her eyes away and turned abruptly back to the view, back to reality.

She didn't want her bones to melt when she looked at Ric. She had to put a stop to such stupidity. It was all very well deciding to forget about reality while she was here, but she couldn't let herself ignore it completely.

She couldn't forget her baby. And she couldn't forget that if she let herself fall for Ric she'd end up in an even worse predicament than she was in already, because Ric wouldn't want her. Then she'd be alone and heartbroken. As it was, she'd just be alone—until the baby came along.

'It's really very beautiful,' she said, just for something to say to cover her awkwardness.

'Would you like a drink before dinner?' Ric indicated the table where he'd been sitting when she found him.

She nodded and moved towards the table. 'Some fruit juice would be nice.'

Several minutes later, she sat sipping ice-cold

juice and letting the view seep into her soul. She didn't think Ric had a clue what had happened to her at the wall and that was a relief. They could continue as before, their casual camaraderie intact.

He stretched his long legs out at the side of the small table and took his phone from his pocket. 'My sisters have sent me a photo.'

He pressed a few buttons then passed the phone across the table.

Lyssa smiled at the picture of two teenagers grinning broadly. It was in extreme close-up and she guessed one of them had been holding the camera phone. They were striking girls with straight black hair and familiar dark eyes. 'They're twins,' she said unnecessarily.

Ric nodded. 'Didn't I say so?'

He hadn't, but she could understand why his uncle and aunt had had their hands full. Being landed with twins must have been a shock and a lot of work. No wonder they hadn't had much time left over for a twelve-year-old boy.

'They certainly look happy,' she said. She should have known Ric wouldn't have done anything to make them unhappy but then, as she passed the phone back to him, she wondered where that thought had come from. She didn't really know him; how could she tell what type of man he was? She'd only met him the day before, yet undeniably it seemed much longer.

'They're beautiful. I can see why you've locked them away.'

He laughed briefly. 'Only one more year and they'll have finished school. I don't know what I'll do with them then.'

'It won't be your decision, will it? They'll be adults.'

'But so young, so vulnerable.'

'It's the twenty-first century, Ric. You have to let young women have their freedom. You can't keep them locked up. There are so many experiences out there waiting for them.'

'Not all good ones.'

'Maybe not, but the majority will be. And the bad ones will make them stronger.'

'I don't like the thought of them having any bad experiences. I want to protect them from all the bad things in the world.'

'I know,' she said softly. 'But they won't thank you for that, I promise you.'

He flipped the phone shut and slid it into his pocket. 'Maybe I don't need thanks.' He looked out over the sea for a long moment, then sighed. 'What would you like to do tomorrow?'

* * *

Lazing on a sun bed the next day, Lyssa gazed up at slivers of blue sky through the rustic roof of sticks that shaded one end of the pool area. Once again, the exact shade of blue eluded her…cerulean? No, too poetic. Cobalt? Too pedestrian. She tapped her chin with the pen, thinking, then squealed as a shower of cool pool water landed on her.

She glared at Ric, trying hard to keep her laughter at bay. 'Is that any way to impress a client?'

He braced his forearms on the tiles at the edge of the pool and his boyish grin made her heart twitch. She sighed. She'd been concentrating on her notepad in an effort to avoid staring at the smooth, hard-muscled planes of his chest as he floated on the pool surface, olive-toned skin gleaming as the sunlight hit droplets of water.

'Why don't you come in for a swim?'

'I'm working.'

As he shrugged she watched the movement of muscles in his toned upper body, his square shoulders.

'You can do that later.'

Yes. Yes, she could. With a huff of breath she tossed the notepad and pen onto a side-table.

She'd tried. She'd really tried to be business-like. But there was a limit to her resistance.

With a glance from side to side to make sure there were no other guests around, she ran across the tiles and, jumping over Ric's head, cannon-balled into the middle of the pool. One effect of an Australian upbringing was that she was completely at home in a swimming pool. She'd spent half her childhood in the water. Well, possibly more than half.

When she came up for air, pushing tendrils of wet hair off her face, Ric was right there in front of her, his grin wide and genuine.

'That's what I call an entrance,' he said, treading water.

'You didn't expect me to climb down the ladder, did you?'

'I don't know what to expect with you, Lyssa. You keep surprising me.'

She ignored the way her stomach flipped over at his words. Especially at the sound of her name on his lips.

'Ladders are for wimps,' she said. 'Race you to the end.' Before she'd finished speaking, she'd lunged into her stroke and was on her way to the end of the pool.

Ric arrived a moment later. 'You cheated. You had a head start.'

She gasped in mock outrage. 'How dare you? I never cheat.'

'All right. I'll race you to the other end.' He pushed off immediately and she had to play catch-up.

She shook her head at him. 'I forgot you soccer players don't know how to play fair.'

He swore in Italian and, laughing, she said, 'OK, let's have a proper race. No head starts.'

He agreed and this time he beat her fairly, but not easily.

She gulped in air as she hung on to the end of the pool. 'That was fun.'

'Yes, it was.'

Ric was right next to her, their shoulders almost touching. He reached out and lifted a strand of soggy hair off her face, smoothing it back with the rest, his touch cutting off her breath.

'I'm glad you're feeling better today.' Suddenly he was serious, his eyes seeking hers.

'Oh, it was nothing.' Her voice sounded strange. She needed to breathe. 'Motion sickness, I guess. Or maybe something I ate.'

'We ate the same foods.'

'Yes.' She cleared her throat and, with an

effort, moved away. 'Motion sickness, then. I think I'll go and sit in the shade now.'

'Good idea. I'll go and fetch us some cool drinks.'

She nodded, then swam for the ladder.

'I thought ladders were for wimps,' he said as he hauled himself up and over the edge of the pool.

'My arms aren't as strong as yours.' She couldn't resist a glance at his well-defined biceps.

He handed her a towel, his eyes skimming over her body as she walked towards him in her wet swimsuit.

'My arms are at your service.'

His smile sent a wave of warmth through her and she had a moment of panic. How was she going to keep her feelings under control if he was going to smile at her like that?

CHAPTER FOUR

AFTER a day spent around the pool having fun with Ric and being entirely too lazy, Lyssa had been thrilled with his suggested itinerary for the next day.

Right now she was waiting for him to organise the boat that would take them along the coast to Positano.

Already today they'd strolled along the main pedestrian street of Amalfi, browsed the many shops selling casual clothes, swimwear, gifts and groceries and had made their way up the spectacular flight of steps to the tenth-century cathedral.

Along the sea front they'd seen the old arsenal, the sixteenth-century Saracen watchtower and the civic museum and from Ric she'd learned much more about the history of the town than she could have gleaned from any regular tour guide. Not to mention that she could listen to his velvety voice all day long.

It had been hard to get her head around the knowledge that Amalfi had been home to more than seventy thousand people during its time as one of the four Sea Republics. It was clearly too small for so many people, but Ric had explained that most of the old city and its population had simply slipped into the sea during an earthquake. She shivered at the chilling explanation.

After sightseeing, they'd lunched in a simple *trattoria*, where Ric had been welcomed enthusiastically by the owners and they'd been served the speciality, a homemade pasta similar to fettucine, with tomato sauce and seafood, followed by susamelli almond biscuits. All very nice.

Catching sight of Ric walking along the jetty towards her, she waved then tightened her stomach muscles in an effort to stop it flipping over.

His long legs, broad shoulders and muscular arms partially revealed by his plain white T-shirt, the sexy one-dimpled smile that appeared when he saw her, all combined to create a truly tempting package. One that made her hormones sit up and take notice, as if his long, powerful body had a chemical effect on her.

Blasted hormones. They couldn't make their minds up, could they? One minute they were reminding her in a gross way that she was pregnant and off the market, then the next they were making her behave as if she was on the hunt for a man.

It wasn't as if she'd just discovered Ric was thoroughly masculine. She'd known from the minute she saw him that he was…well, her fantasy man. But for heaven's sake, he'd be any woman's fantasy man. She didn't have the monopoly on admiring tall, dark and handsome, did she?

But…the lines seemed to be blurring between fantasy and reality. There was definitely more to Ric than she'd originally assumed and the three-dimensional man was a whole heap more interesting than the dream.

What was she thinking?

OK, she could like Ric. It was hard not to like him, but that was absolutely as far as her feelings could go. Because the reality was that he was a man who lived in a completely different world from her, and she was a pregnant woman who had to get her priorities right.

His life was here in Italy and hers was back in Australia.

The circumstances were all wrong and she would be stupid to take any notice of the foolish fluttering in her stomach.

Within minutes she was seated in the motor boat he'd hired for them. Ric grinned like a little boy as the engine roared into life. Typical male, she thought, smiling as he guided the boat out of the small harbour. They did love their toys, didn't they? The more powerful the better. They were just boys inside. But as childish as his enjoyment might be, it felt good to see him so happy.

It crossed her mind that inside Ric might still be the lonely boy he'd been at twelve. But before she could take the thought any further they were flying across the water and Lyssa's hair was whipping across her face, making her wish she'd tied it back. She held it in one hand while she gazed at the beautiful coast, small hotels perched on the cliffside, little fishing towns that couldn't be reached by road, tiny bays and secret inlets. The coast was just as striking from down here on the water as it was from up above.

Their first stop was at Conca dei Marini, a lovely bay where they transferred to a row boat along with a few tourists to enter the Emerald Grotto.

Sitting on Ric's left on the narrow timber seat, Lyssa gasped and grabbed his arm. 'Look!'

The scene before her was dominated by brilliant green and blue lights reflecting off the rock formations that twisted upwards to the roof. It was like a natural fireworks display, and the jewel-like sheen of the water cast an almost holy glow on the walls of the cavern.

With a low chuckle, he said, 'I'm looking.'

'I suppose you've seen it before,' she said, feeling like an idiot and unclenching her fingers from his solid bicep.

He put his right hand over hers and prevented her pulling away. He looked directly into her eyes. 'Yes, I've seen it before, but I never enjoyed it so much.'

Her breath stalled in her throat. Unable to speak, she looked up at the numerous hanging stalactites, thin and delicate, catching the light like chandeliers.

She'd never forget this moment; it was surreal. The beauty of their surroundings, the warmth of Ric's hand contrasting with the cool air of the cave. All she could do was absorb it and know that the memory would stay with her forever.

* * *

From a distance, Positano looked like a bowl of
Neapolitan ice cream, but as they drew closer
the colours separated into houses stacked ver-
tically on the slope of a mountain, with small
paths running down to the beach. No wonder
the town hadn't been spoiled by tourism, she
thought; there simply wasn't room for major
development.

One of the town's major attractions, she discovered, was its vast array of boutiques lining
the narrow lanes and alleyways with their
displays of colourful garments. All very interesting at first, but after a while her eyes began
to glaze over.

And she must have climbed *thousands* of
steps. Where other towns had streets,
Positano had steps.

Flattening her hand against the nearest wall,
she leaned in while dragging a deep breath
into her lungs.

Ric's head dipped to look into her face.
'Are you OK?'

He didn't look any different, drat him, while
she felt sticky and bedraggled, her hair plastered to her face and neck. He was so fit and
she…well, evidently, she wasn't as fit as she
thought she was. Just another reason why he

wouldn't want anything to do with her if they hadn't been thrown together like this.

'Lyssa?' He took hold of her elbow. 'Come on, let's get you out of the sun. Why didn't you tell me you were feeling unwell?'

'I'm not.' She managed to push off the wall. 'Just hot and tired.'

Actually, she was feeling a bit nauseous too, but it wasn't much. Not worth mentioning.

'We'll go and have a cool drink. Come on.'

He kept hold of her arm and it seemed too much effort to drag it away. And really, what was the harm anyway?

When they reached the grand terrace of an immaculate hotel with lemon trees in terracotta tubs between the tables, she fought her instinct and let him fuss over her. She'd never been in a relationship where a man wanted to fuss over her and if this was what it was like, it wasn't too bad at all.

Protective didn't have to mean controlling. It wasn't the same as her brothers dictating whom she should and shouldn't see, it was kind of nice. When Ric got all protective of her, when he looked at her with his dark eyes as if she was important and fragile, and worth caring about, as if it really mattered how she was feeling, well, it was something she hadn't experienced before and she had to admit, she liked it.

She shouldn't have stayed with Steve as long as she had. She should have listened to the little voice that told her she didn't deserve to be in a relationship where she was constantly waiting for him to acknowledge her existence. She'd excused him by saying he was a workaholic but now she could see that, most of the time, he just hadn't wanted her there.

They'd had some good times too. Of course they had—she wasn't a complete idiot. It was the good times that had made her hang around, waiting for the next one.

But his selfishness when she'd announced her pregnancy had finally opened her eyes to his true nature. If she was a different type of person, she'd be full of regrets for having wasted so much time on him. But she didn't put her energy into regrets. And she couldn't regret being pregnant because this was a baby and all babies were special. As much as she would have loved a proper, nuclear family, she knew she'd never regret choosing to bring up her child alone.

After Ric had assured himself that she had sufficient shade and was perfectly comfortable, he finally sat down. 'Will you promise to tell me next time you're feeling ill?' he asked, sounding slightly exasperated.

She nodded before turning away to stare out to sea with unfocused eyes. She'd thought that travelling at this early stage of her pregnancy would make no difference to what she could do but if this was the way it affected her, she'd have to be more careful. She'd have to adjust her expectations. She didn't like the idea of admitting to being a weak female, but it seemed in this she had no choice.

'Those islands you're looking at are the famous ones where the Sirens were said to have lived.'

Lyssa hadn't been looking, but she brought her attention back to the dark shapes in the distance. 'The women with the beautiful voices that no man could resist?'

'Well, there are various stories. They were either nymphs or birds with women's faces.'

'Birds with women's faces. The person who thought up that description must have had a weird imagination. Perhaps he was henpecked.'

Ric laughed, then they lapsed into companionable silence.

After several comfortable minutes, Lyssa asked, 'Your knee doesn't hurt after climbing all those steps?'

'No.'

'So, when are you going back to playing football?'

He swirled the drink in his glass. 'Well, I could go back in time to start training for the new season. It's a couple of months away yet.'

'Why don't you look happy about that?'

He looked up. 'You ask a lot of questions.'

'Yes, I think we established that already. You've been able to answer all of my other questions, why not this one? Is there a problem?'

Sighing, he leaned back, hooking one arm over the chair, which stretched the T-shirt across his chest. 'Yes, there's a problem, but I'm not going to complain to you about it.'

'Why not?'

'Because that's not what you're here for.'

She narrowed her eyes and regarded him thoughtfully. 'Don't they want you back?'

She could tell by the flash of pain in his eyes that she'd scored a direct hit. He stared at the glass-topped table between them without speaking.

'I'm sorry,' she said, her heart going out to him.

'It's not that simple.'

Ric watched the liquid settle in the bottom of his glass once he stopped swishing it around.

He loved playing, but it was more than that and he didn't think Lyssa would understand. In fact, he was sure she wouldn't. How could she when she didn't even like the game?

Giving it up wouldn't just mean no longer pulling on his football boots, it would mean changing his whole lifestyle and he didn't think he was ready to do that. It was all he'd known for his entire adult life.

Training, playing, partying. It was all part and parcel of the life he'd built for himself. The club was like a second family. He had nothing against his uncle and aunt—they had cared for him, but he wasn't their own child. At the club, he'd been the same as everyone else. An equal.

And then there were the women, but he couldn't tell Lyssa about them. They were always there, lurking around the club, easy to find. Women who knew the score. They liked to date footballers for the prestige—and the athletic bodies. They wanted nothing more from him than his stamina in the bedroom and his short-term presence in their lives.

If he left the club…what then?

He'd be alone. Life would be completely different.

Lyssa was still looking at him, her warm brown eyes wide, not laughing now but concerned for him. A woman who cared about him—that was something he hadn't experienced before.

He forced a smile.

She tilted her head in the way she often did when she was questioning him. 'Why is it not that simple?'

'I still have a contract. I can go back.'

'But…?'

He sighed again and put down his drink, rubbing his knee with one hand. 'I'm twenty-eight years old with an unreliable knee. It's been reconstructed twice now. Yes, I could play again and the knee might be fine…or it could break down in the first game. There's no way of knowing.'

She nodded. 'I can understand why you'd be worried about that.'

'It's not a matter of being *worried*.' He shook his head.

'What is it, then?'

'Why would the club take the risk on me? They'd be better to put the development time into a younger player.'

Frowning, she said, 'I don't understand. *Have* they said they don't want you back?'

'They've suggested that I should consider my playing career over and concentrate on my business interests.'

She sucked in a breath through her teeth. 'Is that what you're going to do?'

'No.' He threw up his hands. 'I told you it wasn't that simple.'

'You want to go on playing?'

'I can't give it up.' Rubbing the back of his neck, he spoke in a low voice, as if talking to himself as much as to her. 'I have other interests, but they've only ever been a sideline, not something I want to focus on. I have people running the businesses. I'm not needed. I would only be interfering.'

Glib words of comfort died on Lyssa's lips. She was starting to see his dilemma. He was in a position where there was an obviously right decision and he didn't want to make it. He would go against everything his head told him was right, in order to follow his heart.

'How long have you been at the club?'

He shrugged. 'Ten years.'

So he'd only been a teenager when he'd arrived there. Remembering what he'd told her before, she had a sudden flash of understanding. She reached for his other hand. 'It's the only place you've felt you belonged since your parents died.'

He looked as if he was going to deny her statement, to rubbish it, but he hesitated, searching her face, then his expression changed and he nodded slowly.

'I mean no disrespect towards my uncle and aunt; they are wonderful, generous people and I will always be grateful to them for taking me in…but…' He shrugged.

But the club had been like a family. She understood and her heart lurched for him. He must have been lonely when he went to the club and it had become his substitute family. Now he had to come to terms with leaving it.

She could think of nothing sensible to say so she squeezed his hand instead.

After a long moment he turned his hand over and gripped hers.

Two days later, Ric stole a glance at Lyssa as she sat beside him with her hands over her eyes. Fixing his own eyes firmly back on the twisting road, he continued the slow drive uphill through the Valle del Dragone. He'd promised to tell her when she could remove her hands, when they'd passed the last of the steep ravines on the way to the mountain-top town of Ravello. He'd convinced her it would be worth the drive for the views alone and she'd trusted him.

Lyssa trusted him. It gave him an inexplicable buzz to know that. He'd never felt so protective of anyone—even more than his sisters, and that was saying a lot. Perhaps it was the aura of innocence that hung around her.

Not innocence exactly… What was the word he was looking for? Simplicity. Or honesty. She was the most honest woman he knew. He trusted her too; that was why he'd told her about his dilemma when he'd shared it with no one else. It was strange to think they'd only known each other a matter of days—almost a week now; it felt much, much longer.

Maybe it was because they'd spent most of that time together. Almost every waking moment, in fact. The truth was, even when he wasn't with her, he was thinking about her, wondering what she'd like to do next; whether she was happy. It felt as if several weeks of getting to know each other had been condensed and distilled into this short space of time.

Would it have been the same if she'd been a different person? No, of course not. If she'd been the kind of woman he'd expected her to be, he'd have been gritting his teeth and forcing himself to get through this job for his uncle's sake. Not enjoying every moment of it as he was with Lyssa.

'You can look now,' he said as he drove into the town's narrow medieval streets.

Lyssa dropped her hands into her lap and smiled across at him. 'OK, I survived the drive. This had better be worth it.'

'It will be. I promised, didn't I? Have I let you down yet?'

She shook her head, her long, wavy hair shimmering in the afternoon sun that streamed through the car window. It was that in-between, light brown colour that most women couldn't wait to change. None of the women he knew in Milan had that colour; they would have bleached it blonde or dyed it dark, but he couldn't imagine Lyssa with any other colour.

And true, she looked older and more sophisticated when she straightened it, but he preferred it when she left it natural. He really liked the messy waves; they were more fun, more *her*.

He parked the car—which would have been a challenge any later in the season—and they set off to look around the small, stylish town.

After an abundance of shops in Positano and Amalfi, Lyssa enjoyed the quiet elegance of Ravello's paved streets with its concentration of old churches and *palazzi*.

She was impressed by the cathedral with its marble pulpit and six lions crouched at the base, and when they came back out onto the main *piazza* she noticed the square tower marking the entrance to Villa Rufolo. Ric explained that the thirteenth-century Moorish villa had been a former home of Wagner and he'd written part of his opera *Parsifal* there.

'During the main summer period, the gardens host concerts of Wagner's music,' he said as they passed through the entrance.

'What a pity I'm here too early in the year.'

'Are you a fan of Wagner?'

She gave a wry smile. 'Wouldn't know him if I fell over him, I'm afraid.'

Ric grinned back. 'Nor me. I know very little about classical music.'

'But still, it's so beautiful here, I'm sure the concerts would be lovely, and they're part of the local culture.'

Ric nodded and took her hand as they wandered through the subtropical gardens filled with exotic colours, crumbling towers and luxurious blossoms. It felt natural to have his long fingers curled around hers while she absorbed the beauty around her. The perfume of flowers hung in the air and she took deep breaths, wondering how she'd find the words to write about all she'd found here.

When they'd seen everything they returned to the *piazza* and in a comfortable silence walked east to the larger gardens of the Villa Cimbrone, where they spent more than an hour exploring the temples and grottoes and the geometric rose garden with a sundial in the centre.

They meandered slowly along a wide path in the shade of a wisteria-covered pergola and ended up at the Terrace of Infinity. From there the view of the Gulf of Salerno was simply stunning.

Ric looped an arm around her shoulders as she stood transfixed, absorbing the breathtaking vista, soaking up the special peacefulness about the place.

Apart from the chirping of crickets and the hum of other insects, she heard no sound. They weren't the only tourists in the gardens, she knew. They'd passed people and seen more from a distance, but right now the world seemed to have emptied of all but the two of them. And she'd never found such peace in all her twenty-six years. Certainly not in recent times.

She leaned against Ric, content to feel his solid support, to know he was there for her. His grip tightened slightly and she felt a subtle shift in the atmosphere. It was as if, in that moment, something had changed between them.

The sun had already started to set when Lyssa and Ric strolled back through the little town and entered the twelfth-century *palazzo* perched high on the cliffs—now an exclusive hotel with a reputation for fine dining.

It was like a movie set, she thought, with its abundance of marble, stone lions, palm trees in enormous pots and chic, glittering clientele. She immediately felt out of place amongst these beautiful people and was relieved when, after a quick word with the hotel staff, Ric led her through a series of arches to a large dining terrace lit by lanterns strung from the canvas roof.

The tables, covered in mixed and matched linen in colours of lemon, coffee and white, gave a touch of elegance to the more casual setting.

Seated at a table right at the edge of the terrace, she looked down on the tiny fishing boats a thousand feet below. 'I keep thinking

I've seen the best view possible and then there's another one,' she said with a sigh.

'Wait till the sun goes down,' he said. 'You'll love it. From here the coast looks like a diamond necklace.'

She grinned. 'You're quite poetic for a sportsman.'

He made a dismissive gesture. 'I read it somewhere.'

She didn't believe him. He could try to pretend he didn't have a sensitive side, but she knew it was there—she'd seen the evidence and she suspected he had an inner romantic trying to get out.

She continued to smile as she turned away to watch some fellow diners being served. The aroma of sauces and spices made her mouth water and—after a shocking start to the day with morning sickness now in full swing—she was glad that the smell of food had no effect on her other than to make her hungry.

'I've decided I love to watch Italian waiters at work,' she said after a moment. 'It's as if they consider it a pleasure to serve you. Not like the young waiters in most countries who are doing it as a part-time job until something better comes along.'

'Tell me about living in Australia. Now that

you're grown up, I mean. I already know about your childhood.'

She pulled a face. 'There's not much to say. What do you want to know?'

'Well, for a start, is there anyone…a boy-friend or…anyone?' he asked casually as he picked up the menu.

She opened her mouth to tell him about breaking up with Steve and about her pregnancy. Now was the perfect time, and she wanted to tell him, but conflicting emotions churned inside her.

She recalled the moment on the Terrace of Infinity when she'd felt something shift. Her own feelings were the problem here. She wanted to be honest with Ric, but at the same time, didn't want him to find her less attractive because of her condition. She liked him too much.

'Not at the moment,' she said, then took a sip of water.

His dark brows rose in a question.

'Not for a while.'

She turned away from his dark, searching gaze. She was annoyed with herself for wanting Ric to know she was single. It wasn't as if she was available.

But then, she might as well find out what she

wanted to know while the opportunity existed. Turning back to face him, she asked, 'What about you? Do you have a girlfriend waiting for you in Milan?'

'No.'

Their eyes locked for a moment, then Lyssa looked away. 'Or anywhere else?'

'No. I don't have…relationships of that type.'

Lyssa widened her eyes. 'What on earth do you mean?' He liked women. She was sure of it.

'I mean, I only have short-term…girl-friends…if you can call them that. There would never be anyone waiting for me.'

Frowning, she said, 'Why?'

He shrugged. 'That's all I want. My life is dominated by my career. Well, my career *is* my life.'

'But—'

'The food here is supposed to be really good,' Ric said, tapping the menu. 'The chef has run a top restaurant in London. What do you feel like?'

As hungry as she was, she wasn't ready to leave the conversation there. 'You mean, you never have more than a few dates with one woman?'

'That's what I mean.'

'And that's what you want?'

He sighed. 'It suits me. I don't want a long-term relationship. It would…interfere with my lifestyle.'

'But in the future? You'll want to get married and have children, won't you?'

He shook his head. 'No.'

Now she was glad she hadn't told him about the baby. It would almost certainly have made him look at her differently and she couldn't bear that.

It should make no difference to her. He wasn't a man she should even *think* about getting involved with, but it did make a difference. She couldn't explain it to herself, but it did.

CHAPTER FIVE

'I SHOULD warn you that the accommodation could be quite basic,' Ric said as he drove inland a couple of days later.

Lyssa sent him a mock glare. 'You couldn't have said that *before* we checked out of the luxury hotel?'

'I think it will be worth it for the food alone, but you'll have to be prepared to rough it a little.' He flicked her a worried glance. 'You don't really object, do you?'

'No, of course not. You should see some of the places I've stayed. Not all of my stories have been all-expenses-paid jaunts like this one.'

Ric grimaced. 'Please, don't tell me these things. I don't like to hear about you alone and at risk.'

'You mean you don't want to hear about the time I shared a room with—?'

'No!' He muttered something in Italian under his breath.

'Because you don't want to think about these things happening to your sisters when they escape your protection?'

He shrugged. 'That too. But mainly because I don't like to think of what might have happened to you.'

'The key word being *might*. If I hadn't been able to look after myself. Which I was.'

Anyway, as far as their next stopover was concerned, she could put up with anything as long as she had her own bathroom. Every morning now, she found it impossible to leave the hotel room for the first hour or more. She hoped the morning sickness would settle down soon, but in the meantime she was just lucky it didn't last all day.

She'd jumped at Ric's suggestion that they get off the beaten track for a while and sample some home cooking. *Agritourismo*, he called it. A farm holiday. It had sounded like a great idea and a good way to experience the real culture of the region; she just hoped it wasn't *too* basic.

As it turned out, the farmhouse was a huge, two-storey stone villa surrounded by ancient olive trees. To reach their rooms, Signora

Lunetta, a squat middle-aged lady who owned the house with her husband, led them through a wrought-iron gate into a walled garden. It was shaded by grapevines trained on overhead wires.

There were two small apartments at the rear of the garden, each of them, to Lyssa's relief, completely self-contained. Signora Lunetta seemed gratified by Lyssa's smile of approval and left them to settle in.

The apartment's décor was simple but pleasant. Lots of solid timber and wrought iron. Basic, yes, but not rough. After unpacking a few essentials, Lyssa went outside to sit on one of the wrought-iron chairs on the cobbled communal terrace area. It was peaceful in the shade of the vines and she closed her eyes, listening to birds and insects, until she heard the sound of Ric's door opening.

Smiling over her shoulder, she said, 'It looks like we're the only guests.'

'More food for us, then,' he said as he straddled another of the chairs, leaning his forearms on its back. 'Do you fancy a tour of the farm?'

'Sure. What's the point of coming here if we don't see what it's like? Give me a minute to grab some better shoes.'

She went back inside the apartment to swap

the open sandals for her trainers, then joined Ric and together they went to seek out a member of the family.

They found Giovanni, the middle son of the Lunetta family, helping his father in the milking shed. After a brief discussion with his father, he agreed to show them around and led them outside.

Starting with the natural grotto where they pressed olive oil, he went on to give them an entertaining tour, showing them the herbs and vegetables grown both for home use and for the market, chickens, calves and donkeys and a yard full of horses which he said they could ride if they wanted to.

Lyssa, a city girl, had never been so close to a horse. She liked the look of them from a distance—she even went to the Melbourne Cup most years—but she'd got through twenty-six years without learning to ride and didn't feel inclined to change now.

Giovanni finished off the tour by taking them back to the milking shed, where Signor Lunetta was preparing to return the cows to their field.

In the corner of the barn, tucked safely out of reach of the cows, a female dog was curled in a bed of straw feeding three puppies.

'Oh, look.' Lyssa crouched near the dog, who lifted her head and sniffed.

The sight of the puppies made her teary. Another effect of those pregnancy hormones, she guessed.

'They're so cute.' Actually, she had to admit, the mother wasn't really an attractive dog, but she was gentle, and her puppies were gorgeous. Lyssa stroked the mother and then petted each of the pups in turn.

Giovanni mumbled a few words and moved away to talk to his father.

'What did he say?' she asked, blinking away the tears as she looked up at Ric.

Ric hesitated. 'He said, they're not working dogs so they're no use. They've found homes for all the others.'

She got to her feet. 'Did he say what will happen to these three?'

When Ric gave her a wary look but didn't answer, she felt the tears well up again. This time she knew she wouldn't be able to blink them away. She hurried outside, where she leaned against the barn wall and tried to get herself under control. She told herself not to be an idiot. This was a working farm and she wasn't naïve, but still she couldn't stop weeping.

She'd heard about pregnancy making women emotional. Now she understood what people meant by that. She didn't even have a bump yet, and already she'd changed so much—hunger, tiredness, nausea and now emotions that she couldn't control. She was a mess.

Ric hadn't followed her outside and she was grateful to him for giving her some space. She didn't want him to see her like this.

Several minutes later, he came around the corner of the shed just as she scrubbed the last remaining tears from her face. Rolling her eyes, she said, 'You must think I'm an idiot.'

'No.' He smiled gently. 'It's OK, Lyssa. The puppies have homes to go to.'

She looked up at him. 'Really?'

He nodded, reaching out to wipe with his thumb a tear she'd missed. There was something in his eyes as he did so that made her heart twist in her chest but she couldn't name it. She didn't dare.

She saw him swallow, then he said, 'And the Lunettas are going to keep them here until we can pick them up.'

'We?'

'My uncle and aunt would like to meet you. They've invited you to lunch at their house. My cousins will be there too and they'll take one of the dogs each for their children. We can come back this way in a few days, pick up the puppies and take them to my uncle's house.'

He hesitated. 'If that's all right with you?'

Tempted to throw her arms around his neck, she laughed instead. 'Better than all right. Thank you, Ric. Thank you so much.'

He shrugged. 'I only did it so you wouldn't write a negative article. I didn't want to—as you say—blot my copybook.'

Yeah, sure, that was why he'd done it. Not because he was a kind, sensitive man who cared about the puppies. Or maybe it was her that he cared about. She smiled to herself. Whatever, she wouldn't embarrass him by saying any of this.

'By the way, Giovanni sends his apologies. He didn't mean to upset you; he wasn't thinking. And I'm sorry too. I shouldn't have interpreted his words literally.'

She flapped her hands. 'It's not your fault, nor Giovanni's. I know this is a farm and they don't think of their animals as pets. I know those cute little calves we saw will probably…'

No, she couldn't finish that thought. She stretched her throat while she tried to swallow a lump. These hormones had a lot to answer for.

'Let's go for a walk,' Ric suggested.

She nodded and after they'd been walking in silence for a few minutes, she let out a deep sigh.

Ric studied her. Her skin was flushed from crying, her nose a brighter pink than the rest of her face. But even with that and her watery eyes, she was lovely. He'd seen women cry before and the activity had made them appear unattractive. Or perhaps it was the cause of the tears that made them unattractive—a selfish cause.

But Lyssa…he should have known she'd be soft-hearted; he'd seen signs of her caring nature already, and her tears had touched him. Back at the shed he'd had to fight an urge to gather her in his arms and promise that nothing would ever hurt her again.

It would have been a laughable claim, of course. He had no idea what her future life would be like; he had no control over it. Once she left Italy, she was on her own. Or perhaps not on her own. Either way, he wouldn't be there to protect her.

She gave him a rueful smile. 'I guess I've irrevocably damaged my image, haven't I?'

Frowning, he asked, 'What image?' To his mind, she'd done nothing but show she had compassion for helpless creatures. What was wrong with that?

'The one of me being tough and able to cope with anything on my travels in foreign countries.'

'Ah, that one. Yes, I'm afraid you've shattered it completely.'

She chuckled. 'I don't normally get so emotional.'

With a lift of his shoulders, he said, 'It's not such a bad trait.'

'No, but…' She chewed on her lip, then sighed, frowning. After a pensive moment, she brightened. 'One day I'm going to write a book about the things that have happened on my travels. I mean, the things that didn't make it into my articles because they weren't meant to happen. The out-takes, if you like.'

'I don't think I'd like to read that book,' he said with a roll of his eyes.

She laughed. 'Well, you won't have to because you won't even know it's been published—if it ever is. You'll have forgotten all about me by then.'

They'd arrived back at the horse yard and he leaned his forearms on the gate. 'I doubt it.'

Her face flushed a deeper pink. 'Really?'

'I've never known anyone like you. I don't think you'll be easy to forget.'

She leaned on the gate alongside him, looking at the horses, not at him. 'You won't be easy to forget either.'

Dinner turned out to be the most spectacular meal of the tour so far. The whole Lunetta family as well as Ric and Lyssa congregated in the dark-beamed kitchen and found seats around the heavy, scrubbed table.

Signora Lunetta radiated joy as she brought enormous platters of antipasto to the table, pointing out the farm produce among the fried pastries stuffed with tomato, involtini of aubergine, fresh ricotta and prosciutto, dried courgette, baby focaccia with onions, beetroot cooked with mint, frittata with fresh artichokes and more.

Lyssa was astounded at the amount of work that had gone into the meal, and this was just the first course. She turned to Ric, seated next to her. 'She must have been working all day to do this. I feel so guilty.'

'I don't think there's any need to feel guilty. I'm sure she enjoys having guests here so she can show off her culinary skills. Imagine how she'd feel if you were one of those skinny women who don't eat?'

Good point. 'I'll say in my article that it's important to pack an appetite when you come to stay here.'

She squished the rogue thought that those skinny women he'd mentioned were probably the same ones he found attractive, and set about doing justice to Signora Lunetta's efforts.

The main course of grilled and skewered meats and chicken, rabbit and duck dishes was served with potatoes, savoury doughnuts and a simple salad of green leaves and herbs dressed with olive oil from the little grotto she'd seen earlier.

Conversation flowed as fast as the wine. Lyssa joined in the conversation and avoided the wine. Between Signora Lunetta's lack of English and her own broken Italian, Lyssa tried to convey how much she appreciated her cooking and the work she'd put into dinner. She thought she'd succeeded when she saw the older woman's grin.

Tarts and flans filled with walnuts, apples and pears followed the main course, and by the time coffee was served Lyssa had reached bursting point. She said goodnight then, feeling as if she'd have to roll to bed, she giggled at the mental picture and left the others to their coffee and limoncello.

Ric joined her and she held on to his arm as they made their way through the walled garden by the filtered light of the moon.

'This is the first place we've stayed that doesn't have a view,' she said. 'Well, except for the stars.'

As she looked up at the patches of night sky visible between the vines, she stumbled on the cobbled terrace. Ric steadied her and the feel of his firm hands on her waist made her stumble over her thoughts too.

She expected him to let go immediately she'd regained her balance, but he didn't. He moved behind her and slid his hands further around her waist, pulling her back into his hard body.

She couldn't breathe. Not because he was holding her tightly, but because he was holding her at all.

'They're beautiful, aren't they?'

'Hmm?'

'The stars.'

'Oh, yes.' She dropped her head back and it hit his chest. She left it there while she stared at the sky, not seeing a thing. Too, too aware of Ric's closeness and her own confused feelings.

She wanted to turn around and kiss him. She shouldn't…she couldn't…but she wanted to.

Why did life have to be so complicated?

When she'd left home, meeting someone like Ric was absolutely the furthest thing from her mind. Meeting anyone at all had seemed impossible.

And getting involved with Ric was still impossible. Their lives were so different.

She stepped forward, feeling his hands slide from her waist, missing them straight away.

'OK, well, time for bed. I mean…' She sucked in a breath and shook her head to rid it of an image of Ric and her in bed, sheets tangled, legs entwined. 'I mean, I'll see you tomorrow.'

Ric looked at her steadily. Not smiling. Just looking in a way that made her shiver inside.

She took another breath and headed into the apartment as quickly as her quivering legs could carry her. She closed the door without looking back. She'd been very near to making a fool of herself. Did Ric have any idea what she'd been thinking, what she'd been wanting? Had he wanted it too?

As she lay in bed she could smell earth and flowers through the open window of her room, and hear a chorus of weird animal noises as alien to her as if she'd come from another planet. But rather than the strange sounds, it was her thoughts that kept her awake for hours. Thoughts of Ric.

The next day Ric was disappointed when Lyssa refused to come to breakfast.

He'd been looking forward to seeing her. Every day he learned more about her and the more he learned, the more fascinated he became. She was nothing, nothing, like the women he was used to, but when he looked at her he'd started to see someone he could be very attracted to.

What did he mean, could be? He *was* very attracted to her. But along with the attraction, there was a mess of other feelings that he couldn't sort out.

Not love. Love couldn't be part of the mix. He'd only been in love once in his life and that had been a disaster. It was not something he intended to repeat.

Ever.

Even letting the memory surface for a second was enough to bring him out in a cold sweat.

He'd been a rookie player. He'd been bowled over by a beautiful woman. Valentina. She'd moved on to the next player. He'd learned his lesson. Simple as that.

It had been a hard lesson but he'd taken it on board and he would never put himself in a position where any woman had such power over him again. The power to break his heart—if it was even possible for his heart to break again. He suspected the vulnerable part of his heart had gone for good.

He found Signora Lunetta in the kitchen, where she'd spread out a buffet of cakes and biscuits, homemade jams, fresh and dried fruit.

After he'd eaten, he asked if she'd allow him to take a tray of food back to Lyssa. Only too happy to oblige, she prepared the tray herself, adding a small vase of flowers cut from the tub outside the kitchen door.

He thanked her and carried the tray into the walled garden, where he found Lyssa sitting at the small table on the terrace.

She looked terrible. She hardly ever wore make-up but today she needed it. Her face was pale and blotchy, her eyes bloodshot.

He put down the tray and sat in the other chair. 'You're unwell again?'

She blew out a breath. 'No. I'm fine.'

'You don't look fine.'

'Thanks. You know how to flatter a girl, don't you?'

He made an exasperated sound in his throat. 'What's wrong with you? Do you need to see a doctor?'

'No,' she said, sighing. 'I've had an upset stomach this morning, no doubt because of all the rich food I ate last night. It was a lot, even for me. Speaking of food, what do you have here?' She leaned forward and peered at the contents of the tray.

'Signora Lunetta sent you some breakfast.'

'How nice of her. Pretty flowers too.' She took the plainest biscuit and nibbled on it. 'We have another two days here, don't we?'

'Yes. What would you like to do this morning?'

'I think I'd like to go into the town, village or whatever it is. Is it too far to walk?'

'No, we could walk. Or we could ride.'

'Horses?' She shook her head. 'Uh-uh, I don't ride. Although, if the Lunettas have some bikes, I'd love to ride one of those. It's been ages since I rode a bike.'

Her colour was returning to normal but she still looked tired. 'Are you sure you're strong enough to ride into the village?'

'It's not very far, is it?' She rolled her eyes. 'I think it would be fun to ride a bike.'

He gave a resigned sigh. He'd have preferred to take her by car, then if she became ill he'd be able to take her to a doctor. But if Lyssa wanted to ride a bike, he'd find one for her even if he had to walk into the village to do so.

'I'll see what I can do.' He pushed the tray closer to her in the hope she'd eat some more breakfast, and walked away.

Lyssa watched Ric go, then ate another biscuit. The sickness might have worn off but it had left behind a huge reminder that nothing could happen between her and Ric. As much as she wanted it to—and after last night, she could no longer see the point of denying it to herself— there was just no way.

No chance at all that Ric would be inter- ested in her once he knew she was pregnant. He'd already told her that long-term relation- ships weren't his style. He didn't want marriage and kids. He certainly wouldn't want another man's child.

Not that she'd even consider bringing up a baby in his world.

She groaned aloud.

She knew she should tell him about the baby. She'd probably imagined the look he'd given her last night, but if she hadn't, telling him would put an end to any interest he might have in her.

So she should tell him. And she would. Soon.

CHAPTER SIX

Lyssa giggled as she struggled to make the rickety old bicycle go in a straight line.

'Where did you find this contraption?' she called across to Ric. 'It's older than me. Much older.' She screeched as the bike veered off the edge of the road again.

'Don't distract me.' He put one foot on the ground when his bike wobbled. 'This picnic is so heavy, it takes all my concentration to keep from overbalancing.' He waved a hand at the enormous picnic basket strapped to the back of the bike. 'Signora Lunetta overdid it a little, I think.'

Laughing, Lyssa laid her bike down on the grassy edge. 'Why don't we eat now and lighten the basket?'

Ric looked around then nodded towards a nearby gate. 'In that field. There are no animals, so we should be fine.'

It was a lovely spot for a picnic, Lyssa decided a short time later, surrounded by the subtle scents of wild flowers and thick, soft grass under the blanket which made it a pleasure to sit on the ground. It was warm but the sun was hidden behind light cloud-cover.

After filling up on fat foccacias and tasty pastries filled with dried fruits, Lyssa stretched out on the blanket. 'I need a *riposo*.'

She heard movement and opened her eyes.

'Rest, *bella mia*. I'm going to pack all this away.'

'Don't let me sleep too long.'

Smiling, he touched her cheek. 'I'll wake you.'

His smile and his gentle touch made her heart miss a beat.

His bella?

She knew she was no stunner. Heck, she had a mirror and she knew how to use it. But Lyssa let out a sigh as she closed her eyes again and drifted off to sleep feeling…beautiful.

In the end they gave up trying to ride and pushed the bikes into the pretty little village. It was completely untouched by tourism, since it was well away from the main road, its ancient stone buildings surrounding a *piazza* with a central fountain. The only people outdoors, they sat on the edge of the fountain while they drew breath after the walk and waited for the village to wake up.

Talking, laughing and enjoying the tranquillity, Lyssa wished the day would never end. Ric leaned forward and for a heart-stopping moment she thought he was going to kiss her. But he picked a piece of grass from her hair, and stood up.

'We should look around while we're here.'

'Yes.' She turned her face away, wondering whether he'd seen the hope in her eyes. She'd been more than ready despite knowing she shouldn't even be considering anything so stupid.

Thank goodness she hadn't embarrassed herself by leaning in for the kiss that never came.

It didn't take long to explore the village and they came across a tiny shop that had hams and salamis hanging from the ceiling and dozens of homemade delicacies direct from the owner's kitchen. Ric bought some items out of courtesy for disturbing the owner's afternoon. Lyssa found the place fascinating—not that she needed more food, but it was a glimpse into the culture she'd only skimmed the surface of so far.

* * *

After an idyllic few days at the farm, Lyssa was a little sad when it was time to climb into the car for the next leg of the tour. She'd considered suggesting to Ric that they should stay longer but when the Lunettas mentioned they were expecting more guests as soon as Ric and Lyssa left, she shelved the idea. There simply wouldn't be room for all of them and besides, she didn't want to share this special place with others. She didn't want to spoil the memory of being there with Ric.

She'd built up quite a collection of special moments that she'd be able to recall much later, when she was alone.

'This is Sorrento,' Ric said, interrupting her thoughts.

She sat up straighter, looking around as he drove into the town and parked at the centrally located hotel. It wasn't the farmhouse but it looked pleasant enough. She had to put the farm experience behind her and focus on the present, keep an open mind. It wouldn't be fair to take an instant dislike to a place just because she'd had such a good time in the previous location, as she knew only too well from her line of work.

And besides, Ric was here. That was enough to make any place outstanding.

Her room had a balcony and a view out to sea—the Bay of Naples this time, she realised, thinking about the route they'd taken. They'd crossed the peninsula since leaving the hotel near Amalfi. She could hear Vespas again. Traffic, tourists—the background noise of a resort town. No more cows and horses and the soporific sounds of rural life.

It was late afternoon when she met up with Ric to explore Sorrento. She ran her eye over his casual but well-cut clothes and stifled a sigh. From what she'd seen on this trip, Italians always dressed well no matter what. It was easy to spot the locals from the tourists.

Ric looked great in absolutely anything and the thought ran through her head that she'd love to see him in his football gear. But that would never happen, would it? By the time he went back to the club—if he went back—she'd have returned to Australia.

She didn't want to dwell on the thought—it gave her an ache in the pit of her stomach—so she shook it off and hurried Ric out of the hotel.

Leaving behind the bustling main square of the town for the back streets, they found the remains of buildings from centuries ago, where people had lived before a ravine was filled in to form the *piazza*.

The cathedral they discovered at the end of another little street so narrow only scooters could enter it, and after marvelling at the inlaid wooden doors they went inside to see fabulous statues and decorations.

They wandered down more old streets and through the ancient Greek Gate to Marina Grande, the harbour. After walking from one end to the other, they agreed on pizza for dinner and stopped at a bar overlooking the water.

'I thought I would miss Signora Lunetta's cooking,' Lyssa said when she'd swallowed her first mouthful of pizza, 'but I've just changed my mind. This is fantastic.'

'You're so predictable,' Ric said, laughing.

'No!' She screwed up her face in disgust. 'You think I'm boring?'

'Not boring. I did not say boring.' He reached across the small table and used his finger to flick a string of melted cheese from her chin.

She laughed. 'Boring *and* messy.'

'Fun *and* sexy.'

She caught her breath while her mind zoomed in on that one word. 'Sexy?'

He stopped laughing. He stared at her for a moment as if he couldn't believe he'd said it out loud. Then his eyes flickered over her face and she saw him swallow. 'Yes,' he said firmly. 'You're very sexy when you eat.'

'Good grief, I'm eating most of the time.'

She laughed and was relieved when he joined in, breaking the moment, but Lyssa's heart was pounding. She wouldn't have let him see it for the world, but hearing him say he found her sexy—even if it only applied to meal times—had made her heart lurch and her stomach quiver.

And the gleam in his eyes had made her tremble with raw need.

What was she thinking?

Lord help her, she was thinking that she wanted him to want her. Because she wanted him.

After pizza, they bought *gelati* from the shop next door to the bar. There were more than sixty flavours to choose from. Ric went for walnut and, although it wasn't an easy choice, she settled on chocolate with candied fruit. As they left the shop Ric told her it had been known as the best producer of ice cream on the peninsula for fifty years, and as soon as she tasted hers she could see why. Both the taste and the texture were out of the ordinary.

Slowly they made their way back to the centre of town, climbing about two hundred steps to reach Piazza Tasso, and then took a seat at one of the many pavement cafés to people-watch until Lyssa confessed to being so tired she couldn't see straight.

When Lyssa surfaced the next day, Ric had finished breakfast and was waiting for her in the hotel foyer, reading a book.

She studied his profile, noting the look of total absorption. She guessed this was typical of Ric, that whatever he did he gave it one hundred per cent. She wondered what it would be like to be made love to by him, whether he'd give the same degree of concentration to every touch, every stroke, every whispered word.

For a moment she imagined herself naked beneath him, the object of his attention—and attentions. A delicious shiver ran through her and she realised she no longer had control over her thoughts. They went to places she had no intention of letting them go.

He looked up then, his face transformed by a more than welcoming smile, and the effect on her was instantaneous, a wave of warmth beginning low in her stomach and spreading in all directions.

Moistening her suddenly dry lips, she forced herself forward. 'What's that you're reading? Something good?'

'A guide book to walks in the area. I'd like to try one today. What do you think?'

'Don't you know the area well enough to go for a walk without a guide book?'

'These walks use tracks that existed before the roads were built, and no, I don't know it that well. I've never been to some of the places they lead.'

'Well, in that case, we should definitely go.'

At the edge of town, they started on the walk by climbing steps which were so steep she almost changed her mind, but when they reached the top of the ascent they found a sweet little church with recorded music playing, though it was completely deserted.

Still pulling air deep into her lungs, Lyssa thought of little old ladies making the same climb to attend mass.

'Who would come all the way up here when there are churches in the town?'

Ric shrugged. 'People who have always done it and don't know how to change.'

She gazed back down the steps. 'Sometimes change can be good for you.'

After a moment's silence, he said, 'And sometimes it's too difficult to contemplate.'

Her head jerked up. 'I wasn't talking about your situation, Ric. I only meant…' She waved a hand at the daunting steps. 'I wouldn't presume to—'

'No, I know.' He shook his head as if he wished he hadn't said anything. 'Shall we go on?'

She agreed and from there they followed paths that had been used by locals for centuries, winding their way through olive and lemon groves. They met no one.

The climb was enough to raise the heart-rate but not enough to be difficult and they were able to talk quite comfortably as they went.

Reaching the hillcrest, Lyssa gasped, not just because she needed air but on account of the extraordinary panorama encompassing the coastlines on both sides of the peninsula.

'This is Sant'Agata sui due Golfi,' Ric said. 'So named because you can see both the Bay of Salerno and the Bay of Naples.'

She was quiet for a moment.

'Worth the climb?' Ric asked, turning to look at her.

'Absolutely. I'm just wondering how I'm going to do justice to this whole tour in a couple of pages of writing. The views alone deserve more than that.'

'I'm sure you'll find a way.'

She snorted. 'I don't know what you're basing your opinion on. You haven't even read any of my work.'

'That's true, but you have such enthusiasm for everything you see or do. I'm sure that would come across in your writing.'

'Oh, really? Well, I hope so.' She kept her voice light while her heart was thumping in overreaction to his words. So he thought she was enthusiastic? It was hardly the most romantic of compliments, yet it warmed her right through. In places she'd forgotten about.

She couldn't remember the last time Steve had said anything nice about her. About her work, her looks, her efforts to please him. It was a long time before their break-up, that was for sure. How had she survived so long with him without those little things?

Ric handed her a bottle of water and she drank from it gratefully while he pulled the guide book from his pocket.

'The book suggests continuing on to Marina di Crapolla.'

She sent a spray of water into the air as she burst out laughing. 'You have to be kidding.'

He laughed at her reaction. 'No. That's what it says here, but it also says the descent is "tortuous".'

'Well, tempted as I am by that evocative name, I think I'll give it a miss, if you don't mind.' The sun was high and she was wary of overdoing things. 'But I wouldn't mind a swim when we get back. Not that I missed the pool while we were at the farm, but it seems a shame not to take advantage of it now that we have access to one.'

'Good idea. I'll even let you *try* to beat me in a race again.'

She'd only been thinking of the cooling effect of the water when she said it, but immediately the thought of seeing Ric in his swimming shorts again made her want to hurry back down the hill. The olive skin with its dusting of dark hair, the broad shoulders, the sculpted chest, the flexing muscles…and all wet and glistening in the sun. Her sigh escaped before she could stop it.

'I let you win last time,' she said with a

cheeky smile. 'Now that I've lulled you into a false sense of security…well, watch out.'

He chuckled and pushed the guide book back into his pocket. 'I can't wait.'

The next day Ric watched Lyssa sitting on the bench seat of the small ferry, smiling into the wind, anticipation evident on her face.

He was looking forward to visiting Capri again himself; it had been a few years since he'd made the short trip and this was a good time of year for it, before the crowds of high summer and up to five thousand visitors a day disembarking at the chaotic harbour.

He was *particularly* looking forward to seeing Capri with Lyssa. He saw everything differently when he was with her. He'd meant what he said about her enthusiasm. It was so much a part of her that it rubbed off on those around her. Well, he couldn't speak for everyone else, but it certainly rubbed off on him. She enjoyed life and he was enjoying it through her.

Because of her.

But she wouldn't be here much longer.

He thrust the intrusive thought away as the rugged limestone cliffs of the island appeared on the horizon, startlingly white against the blue sky. He didn't want to think about Lyssa's trip ending, and he did not want to analyse why.

Lyssa waited while Ric entrusted their luggage to a porter's trolley. She hoped they'd see it again, but in the next moment she forgot about the luggage when they boarded the funicular railway along with many other tourists for the slow, gradual ride uphill.

It reminded her of the ride to Victoria Peak in Hong Kong on an earlier assignment, except that it had been foggy that day and the weather was beautiful here on Capri. She couldn't imagine it any other way.

The funicular deposited them opposite Piazza Umberto—the *piazzetta*, as it was called—and as she gazed at the criss-crossing crowds of people she realised that the chaotic harbour had given no hint of the glitz and glamour to be found at the top of the hill.

And there were so many people. If this was the quiet time for Capri, it must be almost unbearable in high season. Almost.

They explored the whitewashed town with its cobbled streets too small for cars, narrow flights of steps between buildings and arches draped with purple bougainvillea.

The streets fanning out from the square were a shopping mecca for the jetset with prices to match. Lyssa stared into upscale shops at an array of jewellery, designer fashions, handmade sandals, bags, and it didn't take her long to become bored with window-shopping. Even if she'd had the money to spend in these stores, she wouldn't have been tempted.

'What else is there to see? This isn't all there is to Capri, is it?'

'No, it isn't. We could walk up to Villa Jovis, the site of a Roman villa.'

'That's more like it,' she said, beaming. 'Let's go.'

'It was built for Tiberius at the end of the first century AD,' Ric said as they wandered the ruins. 'Legend has it that Tiberius built twelve villas here, dedicating one to each of the twelve gods of Olympus. This one was the most magnificent.' With his hands on his hips he shook his head. 'It's hard to believe that from here he ruled the entire Roman Empire. And, reputedly, flung opponents off the cliffs.'

Lyssa stared at the blue vista beyond those cliffs. It was awesome to think of such power. She shivered. Much as she enjoyed hearing about the Romans, she was thankful she was a modern woman and wouldn't be thrown off any cliffs for speaking her mind.

Ric had moved to stand next to her. When another shiver ran through her, he said, 'This breeze is strong,' and wrapped his arm around her shoulders. 'You're cold.'

She opened her mouth to deny it, but stopped. She liked the feel of his arm around her. She really liked it.

She could feel his breath on her cheek, warm in the cool breeze. She turned her head to look at him and, for a long moment, he stared into her eyes. Voices behind them made them spring apart.

Fifty or more Italian schoolchildren, arguing and talking into mobile phones, made a lot of noise. By tacit agreement, they turned from the ruins and headed back towards town, passing on the way some fabulous houses, most of them partially hidden by white walls topped with vibrant oleander. Lyssa pretended to be terribly interested in the houses. It gave her an excuse not to look at Ric until she'd sorted out her thoughts.

Had Ric thought about kissing her?

From the intense look in his eyes, she'd have said so, but she could be wrong. There had been other moments when she'd felt they were close to kissing and nothing had happened. Would it have happened this time if they hadn't had company?

She didn't know. She hadn't known Ric long enough to be sure one way or the other, but did time have much to do with it? How long did it take to really know someone? Was it even possible? She'd been with Steve for two years and believed she knew him, but she could not have predicted his reaction to her pregnancy. Time had nothing to do with it. Didn't she already feel closer to Ric than she ever had to Steve?

She nodded. It was true. Then, sensing Ric glance across at her, she said, 'Nice house,' and sent him a quick smile.

'Yes, it is.'

Adrenalin was still rushing through her body in tremors, provoked by that instant of locked eyes, that brief connection, the reflection of her own awareness in Ric's eyes.

She knew all the reasons why she should stay away from him and they were numerous. Yet still, if the chance arose, she would not back away from kissing Ric. She would grab it, just to find out what it would be like to be kissed by him, to be held in his arms.

There, she'd made a decision. No more doubts. Just to satisfy her curiosity, she'd seize the moment. Then he'd go back to his world full of beautiful women, and she'd go back to hers. To the reality of raising a child alone. But at least she would have her memories.

Lyssa could see why Ric had insisted it was important to spend a night on the island. Not that she'd needed convincing. A late-evening stroll around the *piazzetta*, which was enclosed by a baroque church and several cafés, was simply magical without all the daytrippers milling about.

And the terrace near the bell tower provided a stunning view of the lights of the Bay of Naples. It was a pity they were only staying for one night. She could get used to this.

They ate at a pretty terraced restaurant where Lyssa tried the island's own speciality, insalata caprese—tomato slices interleaved with buffalo-milk mozzarella and sprigs of fresh basil, drizzled with local olive oil and lemon, and sprinkled with black pepper. She loved the creamy texture of the cheese and followed the salad with black pasta—homemade pasta cooked in squid ink—a dish she'd heard of but never had the nerve to try. But she was in the mood for new experiences. This one was better than she'd expected.

As usual, conversation flowed. In a rare break, Lyssa allowed herself to think about Steve, or, rather, about the meals they'd shared. It had never been like this with him.

Now that she thought about it, they hadn't talked much at all. The exchange of essential information couldn't really be called conversation.

Why had she never realised that when she was with him?

Because she hadn't had anything better to compare it with, had she?

In all the time she'd known him, she'd never experienced her stomach fluttering at the sound of his voice or flipping at the sudden appearance of his smile. She'd never felt a sense of loss when he was out of her sight, or a ripple of excitement when he returned.

Now she knew what it was like to experience all these things and she was a little ashamed of herself. That she, a strong, independent woman, should have settled for so long for a relationship that was less than she deserved.

Because she deserved someone who enjoyed talking with her. Someone who teased and joked, but who always made it clear he valued her opinion.

Someone like Ric.

He certainly wasn't the man she'd thought when she first met him. He didn't fit the mould she'd tried to squeeze him into. He wasn't the arrogant, self-obsessed playboy she'd assumed, even though he had that lifestyle.

But she couldn't have Ric. She was only in Italy for another week. She could enjoy his company while she had it, then she had to walk away as if she'd never met him.

The next day, Lyssa set off with Ric to visit the fourteenth-century Certosa de San Giacomo. When they arrived, it was completely empty.

Hesitant about entering, she gave Ric an uncertain glance. 'You'd think there'd be a caretaker or something. It seems a bit spooky that there's no one here at all.'

'Spooky?' He took her hand, laughing, and led her inside. 'I won't let anything happen to you, Lyssa.'

'I know.' It wasn't the first time he'd said it and she believed him. She wasn't seriously scared, but if she had been, his reassuring grip on her hand would have fixed that. She let him lead her into the former Carthusian monastery turned art gallery.

When they'd finished their visit they continued walking, still holding hands, until they reached the lush Augustus Gardens.

Ric tugged her towards the terrace which overlooked the southern shore of Capri. 'You must see the famous Faraglioni Rocks while you're here.'

She stumbled and Ric reacted quickly, turning and catching her around the waist with his free arm. He held her while she slid her heel back into the trainer that had half fallen off.

Laughing at her clumsiness, she looked up, and the laughter evaporated at his expression, at the look in his dark eyes. An intense look. More than just concern that she might have fallen. So intense that it penetrated deep inside her and made her feel as if he really cared.

It warmed a place she'd only just realised was cold. Her heart?

She became conscious of his arm tightening around her waist and her stomach lurched as he stepped closer. She'd told herself she'd grab the chance, but now it seemed to be here she was scared, frozen by doubt.

But then he smiled at her, and it was a smile she'd come to know so well. More than know— it was a smile she'd come to…love?

She didn't know what to think. Somehow her

arms found their way around his neck and she sighed when he pulled her closer still. Then she *couldn't* think, except about one thing only—the sensation of his lips on hers, and they were moving slowly, teasingly. It was a gentle, sweet, slow kiss. The kiss she'd waited her whole life for.

Her fantasy kiss. From her fantasy man. The image she'd carried in her head all those years merged with reality.

His lips left her mouth and trailed across her cheek. *'Cara,'* he murmured into her hair. 'Lyssa, *bella*, I've wanted to hold you like this.'

She'd wanted it too. She realised now just how much she'd wanted it.

He found her lips again and she melted into him as his lips firmed and he took the kiss deeper. So deep she found herself drowning in sensations she'd never experienced.

She felt sexy. She felt feminine. She felt wanted.

Whatever happened afterwards, she'd never regret this kiss.

Ric held Lyssa away from him and searched her face for some sign she regretted the kiss. But he saw none. He didn't regret it either. He'd been so desperate to kiss her he hadn't been able to resist any longer—and now he couldn't even remember why he'd considered her off-limits.

She was a guest of his uncle's business.

Well, there'd been nothing businesslike about that kiss. He'd done a lot of kissing in the past. Too much, maybe. But nothing had ever been so amazing. So intense. So…different.

Confused by the emotion that swamped him suddenly, he lifted his head and gazed around the gardens. They weren't alone. It had felt as if they were the only people in the world for a while, but he had to pull himself together. He glanced at his watch. They'd have to check out of the hotel soon if they were going to catch the ferry back to Sorrento.

'We should go,' he said.

Lyssa nodded, then her small shy smile turned into a grin. Grinning back, he took her hand and they started walking. No, she wasn't his normal type, but where was the harm?

Clearly this attraction was mutual, and they were both adults, so why shouldn't they have some fun with it before she left?

CHAPTER SEVEN

Lyssa took the cardboard box from Ric and settled it on her lap. 'Oh, look, they're so cute.' She stroked the puppies, which seemed to have grown already.

Ric leaned into the car and kissed her on the lips before closing the door and walking around to the driver's side. She closed her eyes and made the moment last as long as possible.

Every kiss since that first one in the Augustus Gardens the day before had made her fall further into the danger zone, into feeling far more for him than she knew she should. Each touch of his lips had made her want more.

He was a brilliant kisser, no doubt about that. And no doubt he had a heck of a lot more experience than she had. He'd be used to women who were just as experienced.

Not that she would have known from the way

he kissed her. He made her feel special. He certainly hadn't given her the impression she was one of many.

She'd expected just one kiss, but as soon as it had happened she'd wanted more. One wasn't enough. And now, after they'd kissed at every opportunity, she knew no number would be enough. She'd never reach a stage where she'd had enough of Ric.

She turned to wave to Signora Lunetta as Ric drove away from the farm. This was the last time she'd see it and she wiped tears from her face as she twisted to catch a final glimpse.

They were leaving the peninsula for the hills of Campania and she couldn't help feeling regret. Whether she ever saw the Amalfi Coast again or not, she'd never experience it in quite the same way again.

It was everything she'd heard and more, but then her enjoyment of it had a lot to do with Ric. She'd have to bear in mind when she wrote her article that others wouldn't see the region with the same eyes. She'd been falling in love and that had to make a difference, to make the colours more vivid, the scents sweeter.

Yes, she'd admitted it. She'd fallen in love here. She'd passed the point where she could deny it, and she didn't even want to do so any longer. She wouldn't tell Ric, she had more sense than to do that. She knew he saw their kisses as nothing more than, well, kisses. And she knew they'd part forever when she flew out at the end of the trip. Relationships and children weren't on his agenda.

Hearing laughter as she got out of the car, she gave Ric a questioning look across the roof.

'Sounds like everybody is here before us,' he said as he took their cases from the front of the car.

'Everybody?'

'My cousins and their families.'

'Oh.' From the noise, she'd thought it must be the whole village. She was pleased that she'd meet his cousins as well as his uncle and aunt. It would be a good opportunity to find out a little more about Ric.

'Can you manage that?' He nodded at the box she was carrying.

'Sure. It's not heavy.'

'OK. They'll be around the back.'

Carrying their luggage, he led the way down the side of the house, a solid grey stone building surrounded by flowers. The noise level increased when they rounded the corner of the house and, as Ric deposited the cases by the back door, he was spotted.

'Ricardo!'

Several children ran to him. Surrounding him, they competed loudly for his attention and it was a moment before he could detach himself and move back to where she was standing. He reached into the box and removed a puppy with each hand.

Excited children reached out to take them from him.

'Attento, attento.' He handed over the puppies one by one with strict instructions on their care, coming back for the third one and repeating himself patiently.

Enthralled by the way the children obeyed him without question, she was still standing there, holding out the empty box like an idiot, when the adults came over as a group.

Ric took it from her and tossed it aside as he introduced his uncle first. She held out her hand and he shook it respectfully. Alberto Rossetti reminded her of her father and she took to him instantly.

Maria kissed her on each cheek, then enveloped her in a warm hug. 'We thought you were Australian,' she said.

'I am. I was born in Australia.'

'No, no, you are Italian,' she said and, without explanation, took over the introductions.

When Lyssa had met her three sons—Marco, Luca and Gianni—and their respective wives, Maria ushered her over to the stone-paved area beneath an ancient olive tree, where a large table was set for lunch and another, lower table had been placed ready for the children.

Ric's three cousins must have several kids each, she thought, judging by the number of them running around.

'Please, sit.' Maria flapped her hand at the nearest chair. 'In a moment we will talk, but first I have to look after the meal.'

'No problem.' Lyssa did as she was told and before long everyone was seated, except Maria, who had bustled off to the kitchen.

Ric was on her left and she smiled at him. 'The puppies are popular.'

'Yes, they are. It was a good idea of yours.'

'Mine? It wasn't my idea.'

He shrugged. 'The children seem to think so.'

'Because you told them it was.' She shook her head, laughing.

'So, how has the tour been so far?' Gianni asked from across the table. 'Has Ricardo behaved himself?'

Heat filled her cheeks and she felt sure Gianni would know exactly what her blushes meant.

She cleared her throat and made an effort to sound professional. 'It's been an excellent tour. Ric is very knowledgeable about the region. His comments have been both entertaining and educational.'

Ric's dark eyebrows rose. 'You don't have to give me a good report. I don't mind if I lose the job. In fact, I expect to.'

'Yes, well, I know, but…it's true.'

'Ricardo helped us out of a difficult situation,' Alberto said in an apologetic tone. 'Our regular driver, Gino, was unavailable. I hope the change has not caused you inconvenience?'

'No!' She shook her head. 'I meant what I said. The tour has been great. So has Ric. Ricardo,' she corrected, having noticed that none of his family used the shorter name. 'He's a very good tour guide, especially since it's not his real job.'

His cousins laughed.

'You know what Ricardo does for a living?' Marco asked.

'Yes, she knows.' Ric sounded resigned.

'That's not a *real* job either.'

'He plays games for a living.' Luca threw up his hands, laughing.

'Leave Ricardo alone,' Maria said, returning to the table. 'You are always teasing him, you boys.'

'My brothers always make fun of my job too.' Lyssa joined in the laughter.

'You are hungry, Lyssa, yes?'

'Lyssa is always hungry,' Ric said. 'She has an appetite even you would approve of.' He turned to Lyssa. 'You'll soon find that my aunt Maria's culinary skills rival those of Signora Lunetta.'

Lyssa smiled. She hoped so. She was ravenous again. She'd had to skip breakfast and the morning sickness seemed to be getting worse. But the good thing was that she had loads of room to spare for lunch and it sounded as if she might need it.

While Maria served the traditional pasta and there was much noise and laughter around the table, Lyssa took the opportunity to observe Ric's interaction with his family. It puzzled her because these people seemed to care a great deal for him. They teased and scoffed and argued, but he gave back as good as he got—and that was what loving families did anyway. She knew that well enough.

Why, then, had he needed to join the football club before he felt he had a family?

She pondered as she ate, then looked up

when Luca's wife, Emilia, pulled a magazine from her bag and flipped it open. 'Hey, Ricardo,' she called across the table, 'there's a photo of you in this magazine.'

Lyssa heard his groan and, glancing at his face, saw his eye-roll before she turned back to watch Emilia. Finding the page she wanted, Emilia placed the publication, open, in the centre of the table.

Luca grinned at Ric. 'Another model? Or a B-grade actress looking for exposure?' He twisted to get a better look. 'Plenty of exposure by the look of it,' he said, laughing.

Lyssa couldn't see and, unable to contain her curiosity, she leaned forward. In the full-page picture she saw Ric, looking unbelievably gorgeous in a black suit, his arm around a striking woman who was wearing a garment that could nearly be called a dress.

She knew it shouldn't, but the image sent a stab of jealousy into her gut, and it sliced deep.

What on earth had she expected?

She knew what his lifestyle must be like. She'd known there would be women and they'd be beautiful, stylish women. She'd known that ever since she met him. It was all part of the world he lived in, and how could he not be surrounded by adoring women when he looked the way he did?

Besides, there was no understanding between them, no promises, no reason at all for her to believe she had any entitlement to jealousy. They'd shared a couple of kisses, that was all. Mind-messing, dream-invoking kisses, true, but their relationship went no further than that.

'Put it away, Emilia,' Ric said flatly.

'Not going to tell us about her, Ric?' Luca said. 'You won't even let us have a little vicarious fun?'

'It's an old picture. It was taken last season. Before my injury.' He stretched across the table and flicked the magazine closed.

Lyssa glanced at him, saw his frown and wondered what he was thinking, whether he was missing all those women, or whether he was thinking about the lifestyle he'd have to give up if he left football.

She hadn't thought about that before. It wasn't just the camaraderie of the club he'd be deprived of, but everything associated with the job. The fame, the social life, the women…

And then…and then…maybe there'd be a chance for her? Maybe they'd be able to make a life together away from football?

After a moment of soaring hope, her thoughts came crashing back to earth.

What an idiot!

How could she have forgotten that there would be no future at all for her and Ric? It was too late. She was pregnant with another man's baby.

Ric didn't want children at all. He certainly wouldn't want to take on someone else's child.

She was glad she didn't need to contribute to the conversation because at that moment she couldn't have said a word, her throat was so tight.

'That magazine,' Maria said with a disparaging grimace. 'It publishes nothing but gossip. Why can't they publish something about the good that you do, Ricardo?'

Ric waved away her question, shaking his head.

'Because nobody knows about it,' Gianni said. 'He doesn't want them to know.'

Maria murmured to herself for a moment, then turned to Lyssa. 'He was always such a good, kind boy. He still is.'

Lyssa gave her an encouraging nod, still unable to speak.

'He started a football club for boys who have nothing else. Teenagers. Young people at risk of getting into trouble. He gives them something good to focus on instead of crime and violence.'

Lyssa couldn't say she was surprised. She already knew there was more to him than the pleasure-seeking playboy.

'Aunt Maria, please.' Ric sounded exasperated. He tried to change the subject, but Maria persisted.

'I don't understand why you want to keep it quiet,' she said to him before turning back to Lyssa. 'He pays for everything, you know, but these magazines, they make it sound like he does nothing but go out womanising and attending frivolous parties.'

'Well, he does a lot of that too,' Luca said, chuckling.

Ric's shrug was eloquent. Lyssa knew he couldn't deny it and she didn't expect him to. But sooner or later, he'd leave that life behind. Sooner, if he made the decision his club wanted him to make.

Just then, a baby's cry coming from the far side of the tree made them all stop to listen. Marco's wife, Nina, got up from her seat at the end of the table, wheeled a pram over, parked it next to her chair, then leaned in and picked up a very young baby.

'Oh.' Lyssa breathed out the word. 'A baby.'

'My newest granddaughter,' Maria said proudly. *'Mia piccina.'*

'She's so small.'

'That's because she is only three weeks old,' Nina said as she sat down with the baby cradled in her arms.

Marco moved closer to his wife and slid an arm around her shoulders while he used his other hand to stroke the baby's cheek. Her cries stopped.

Lyssa envied the obvious bond between the parents. As she watched the loving picture of Marco hugging his wife and caressing his daughter simultaneously, she became conscious of an acute sense of loss on behalf of her own baby. He or she wouldn't have parents who loved each other and both adored their child.

Tears clogged her throat and prevented her from answering when Nina looked over and asked, 'You would like to hold her, Lyssa, yes?'

She nodded, silently cursing the pregnancy hormones that made her so frustratingly emotional. Nina placed the tiny pink bundle in her arms and she just stared at the beautiful baby girl, wondering whether her own child would be a girl too. For some reason she felt it would.

What would she look like? Not that it made any difference; she'd love her regardless. Or him, of course.

Relaxing a little, she bent her head and sniffed the baby's skin. It smelled sweet, of milk and powder and pure baby.

'Do you want children, Lyssa?'

She started at Nina's question, her head jerking up. 'Yes, of course,' she said automatically. Then, unable to resist it, she turned to Ric. 'You're crazy to say you don't want children.'

He looked startled.

'How could you not want something so adorable? How could you turn your back on the chance to know your son or daughter?'

Reminding herself that he was not Steve, that he hadn't walked out on her and the baby, she bit her lip before she said something completely undeserved.

'I'm happy as I am,' he said.

Maria made a derisive sound as she started to collect plates. 'He says that now, but he will want children one day. When he finds the right woman and marries her.'

'I'm not going to marry,' he said.

Ignoring him, Maria leaned over to kiss the baby then headed for the house.

Lyssa thought about the way the children had swarmed around him when they'd first arrived. They obviously adored him and he'd been great with them. And he was Italian. She'd never met an Italian yet who wasn't family-oriented.

Was his denial somehow connected to the death of his parents? She'd heard of people who'd grown up as orphans and then didn't want to have children in case they died and left them alone. But Ric had grown up as part of this loving family. Without his parents, yes, but still loved.

She couldn't figure it out, but instinct told her he would be a fantastic father and his kids would be very lucky. A heck of a lot luckier than her baby, that was for sure.

But she'd learned her lesson with Steve. It seemed some people just did not want to be parents.

She hoped Ric would change his mind one day, as Maria said. With the right woman. She had to close her eyes and concentrate on dealing with a surge of sadness at the knowledge that it wouldn't be with her. For a moment, it threatened to overwhelm her, but she forced it away. She'd deal with it later.

Opening her eyes, she caught Ric looking at her with concern.

'Are you feeling all right?'

'Perfectly.'

He continued to frown for a moment, then Nina held out her arms to take the baby, saying something about changing and feeding her. Lyssa had no choice but to hand her over.

'You look unhappy,' Ric said once she was settled again.

She made an effort to smile. 'I'm not. I'm having a great time.' She looked around at the garden and realised she couldn't see the end of it. 'How large is this property?'

'Quite large. The boundary is beyond the orchard.' He gestured towards the fruit trees she could see in the distance. 'We'll go for a walk later, or maybe tomorrow.'

They planned on staying at least one night. Ric had assured her his uncle and aunt would be pleased, although she didn't like the idea of causing them extra work.

'Perhaps I should go and offer to help Maria,' she said, looking over her shoulder at the sturdy stone house in time to see Maria and Gianni's wife emerge with trays of food. 'Oh, too late.'

She'd thought the pasta was the main course, which was why she'd made a pig of herself with a second helping, but she was wrong. Maria had cooked pork fillet with roasted peppers, aubergine croquettes with tomato sauce, lemon-scented veal meatballs and potatoes with chilli and pecorino.

While she ate, Lyssa chatted to Maria about all the wonderful food she'd had on her trip and how she would struggle to do it justice in her article.

'Do you cook, Lyssa?'

'No.' She sighed. 'Not the traditional dishes anyway. Not the complicated stuff like this.' She waved a hand at the remains of the meal on the table. 'I can do enough to get by. I know the basics.'

'You're like most young women,' Maria said. 'More interested in a career than cooking.'

'It's the same here in Italy?'

'Oh, yes. My sons' wives have their families now so they don't work so much, but they don't spend much time in the kitchen either. I adore them all; they're good wives and mothers, but things are different now. Their priorities are different. They're not interested in learning the old skills.' She sighed. 'And when my girls come home from Switzerland, they won't want to know either.'

The wistful look on Maria's face made Lyssa's chest tighten. She hadn't missed that

Maria had called Ric's sisters *my girls*. There was definitely more love in this family than Ric had led her to believe.

As for passing on her culinary knowledge, it seemed things had changed everywhere and, as much as her parents would find it hard to accept, the world had moved on. Still, she couldn't help thinking it a shame that skills as precious as Maria's would disappear.

Salad, dessert and then lots of fresh fruit followed, all interspersed with masses of conversation in both languages around and across the table. She was becoming more fluent in Italian and was really enjoying the company of Ric's family. When she looked at her watch she saw they'd been having "lunch" for five hours.

Eventually, when no one could eat another mouthful, Alberto brought a CD player from the house and put on some music, then he held out a hand to Maria and the two of them began to dance.

Lyssa looked at Ric and her eyebrows lifted.

'This is normal,' he said, grinning. 'In a moment, all the others will be dancing too.'

'And you?'

'No, this is usually my cue to disappear.'

'Oh.' She turned away, disappointed. But

then she changed her mind and twisted back to face him. 'But you can dance, can't you?'

Marco overheard her question as he led Nina towards the impromptu dance floor. 'Of course he can. My mother made sure all of us boys could dance before we grew up. She considers it more important than reading and writing. But we can do that too,' he said over his shoulder.

'So…' She tipped her head to the side and did a deliberate flutter of her eyelashes. 'Dance with me?'

He smiled. 'Since you ask, I can't say no, can I? It's my job to keep you happy.'

'Absolutely right.'

It was even better than she'd imagined, dancing with Ric. Her dreams would be filled with this dance for years to come. She just knew it.

And it took all her will-power not to forget where they were. Because if they'd been alone…

After several minutes, Ric brushed his cheek across her hair and whispered in her ear, '*Lyssa, bella.*'

She lifted her eyes to meet his. What she saw made her breath stutter.

'Shall we go for that walk now?'

She glanced at his uncle and aunt, still waltzing, so light on their feet for people of their age.

'They'll be occupied for ages yet,' he said. 'They won't notice we've gone. Come on.'

Strolling across the lawn, his arm around her shoulders, Lyssa felt her heart start to race. She knew the cause.

Anticipation.

She desperately wanted Ric to kiss her again. She wanted to feel his lips, to taste his mouth. And his look had told her he wanted it too.

As soon as they were out of sight of the dancers, Ric stopped, took her in his arms and bent his head to touch her lips lightly with his.

She moaned.

His lips firmed and coaxed hers apart. At the first stroke of his tongue against hers, her knees gave way. He held her close, then backed her against a tree and she leaned into it, grateful for its support when Ric kissed her again.

This time he explored her mouth thoroughly, and she let him, doing some exploring of her own. He tasted of the wine she'd declined earlier and it was intoxicating. She did feel a little drunk when she finally came up for air.

He nuzzled her neck, murmuring soft words she couldn't distinguish but which made her feel wanted, desired.

'Ric,' she said between shivers, 'your family is not far away.'

'Far enough.' He covered her lips again and kissed her deeply, his tongue thrusting into her mouth, leaving her in no doubt where his thoughts were going.

Hers were on the same track but one of them had to be sensible and, when his hand found her sensitive breast through her T-shirt and squeezed it gently, she knew she had to be the one, and soon.

'Ric…no.'

'Lyssa, cara…'

She weakened when his fingers moved slowly in caressing circles and dropped her head back against the tree, moaning with pleasure, but then she remembered where they were and caught his wrist.

'No, Ric, please. Not here with your family near by.'

He stopped immediately. 'No, you're right.' Resting his cheek against her hair, he breathed deeply. 'To be continued.'

She gave a soft laugh and he dropped another brief kiss on her parted lips. 'You are too tempting,' he said before straightening away from the tree.

She laughed again. 'I don't know about that but you're pretty tempting yourself.'

Taking her hand, he tugged her against his side. 'When we're alone I'll show you how tempting you are.'

Her muscles turned to jelly as she let her imagination run away with that thought.

Then he sighed. 'But now we should go for that walk.' He led her along a well-worn track between rows of trees.

'You have a lovely family,' she said after they'd walked for a while.

'They're good people.'

'Good people who think the world of you.'

'They're very generous.'

She gave him a curious look. He didn't seem to realise how much they cared about him. He thought they were just being kind. Sure, they were generous, but they clearly felt they got something in return for their generosity, and that was having him as part of their family.

In a moment of clarity she saw past the façade of the confident man who escorted models and actresses to sophisticated venues, to the lonely little boy who thought he didn't belong anywhere.

Chewing on her bottom lip, she wished she

knew the right thing to say. She suspected he'd resisted giving these people his love from fear that they'd be taken from him. Just like his parents.

He cared about them, that much was obvious, as was his gratitude, but it was also evident that he had kept a part of himself closed off. And that was a real shame in her opinion.

'Your uncle seems to appreciate that you helped out by driving me.' And what a lucky day it had been for her when their regular driver had crashed his car.

'Yes, he does. The business means a lot to him; he would hate to let anyone down.' He shrugged. 'But he works too hard. I wish he'd retire.'

'Why doesn't he?'

Ric took a slow breath and let it out again before speaking. 'This is only my supposition. I think he is reluctant to let the business go because he always hoped one of his sons would take over from him, but they've all gone off in their own directions. None of them has the slightest interest in taking it on but my uncle is still living in hope.'

'What about you?'

'Me?'

She looked up at his incredulous tone. 'Couldn't you take it on? You said you have business interests outside football. Couldn't you add this one to them?'

'Well, I'm not one of his sons.'

'Irrelevant, I would have thought.'

'How can you say that? There's a huge difference between a son and a nephew.'

She honestly didn't think his uncle and aunt saw it that way, but then, she could be wrong.

'Besides, I have people managing my other businesses for me. It wouldn't be right to put someone in charge of my uncle's business. That is not what he wants.'

'No, I see what you mean.' But she couldn't help wondering whether Alberto was hanging on to the business in the hope that Ric would take it over when he retired from football. Again, she could be wrong, but her instinct told her she was closer to the truth than Ric.

CHAPTER EIGHT

THE next morning Lyssa only just made it in time to the shared bathroom. She felt guilty for hogging the room for so long but she had no choice. She was stuck there until the sickness eased off enough for her to think about doing anything else.

When there was a knock on the bathroom door, she closed her eyes and prayed it wasn't someone in desperate need.

It was Maria. 'Are you all right, Lyssa? Can I help you?'

'I'm fine,' she called back. 'I'll be out in a moment. I'm sorry to keep you waiting.'

'Take all the time you need.'

Eventually she felt able to step into the shower and then she pulled on her jeans, noting that the zip was a bit difficult to fasten. It wouldn't be long before she'd have to think about bigger clothes, or at least stretchy ones.

Her T-shirt hid the tightness of her jeans and she gathered her things together before opening the bathroom door.

Maria was dusting a small table opposite the bathroom and she turned immediately, her eyes dropping to Lyssa's stomach then lifting to her face with a questioning look.

Lyssa didn't know what to say. She swallowed and decided to act as if there was nothing unusual in a guest throwing up for an hour, hoping Maria wouldn't ask outright the question that was in her eyes. 'Good morning,' she said brightly.

Maria smiled indulgently and came towards her, kissing her on both cheeks again. 'Good morning, Lyssa. You are better now?'

'I'm fine, thank you.'

Nodding, Maria stepped back and patted Lyssa's arm. 'It will pass.'

Lyssa said nothing but she felt her cheeks heat up. Could she be any more transparent?

After a moment's silence, Maria said, 'Ricardo is with his uncle. If you have nothing else planned, I thought you might like to help me in the kitchen. You might learn a thing or two about cooking.'

Lyssa grinned. 'That's a great idea. I'd love to.'

'We have some guests arriving today. A family from England. I want to prepare a nice meal for them for tonight.'

'Just give me a minute to tie back my hair and I'll be there. I can't wait.'

Later that morning, Ric approached the house with his uncle. They had been walking and talking about the tour business. His uncle seemed to value his opinion, though the reason escaped Ric when he had three sons to turn to—Marco, a lawyer, always ready to offer advice whether wanted or not, Luca with his creative talent and Gianni, the practical one. So why would he care what a mere footballer thought of his plans?

Arriving at the back of the house, he reached for the doorknob and entered the kitchen. He heard laughter as he stepped inside and stopped abruptly, stunned by the sight of Lyssa working at the large table with his aunt. Cooking, it appeared.

She was flushed and had something red smeared across her cheek but, if the smile on her face was anything to judge by, was enjoying herself immensely.

Lyssa looked up and her smile stretched even

further. His chest tightened with hope that it meant she was pleased to see him.

Not as pleased as he was to see her though. He'd grown used to her being a late riser, staying in her hotel room till mid-morning, but lately he'd found himself counting the minutes till she appeared. And after their kiss last night, the waiting had been even worse this morning.

'Maria's teaching me to cook.'

'Really?' He didn't want to analyse why, but seeing her working with his aunt gave him a strange, warm feeling. He'd never brought any of his girlfriends to meet his relatives. The very idea was ridiculous. They'd have nothing in common, and Maria would not like the self-centred women he dated in Milano.

Maria must like Lyssa a lot because she shared her kitchen with no one and here she was, laughing along with Lyssa and looking happier than he'd seen her for ages. Come to think of it, she'd never *had* anyone to share her kitchen with. Perhaps she'd been waiting for someone like Lyssa to come along.

But Lyssa wasn't his girlfriend.

Maria turned to the stove and stirred the contents of a deep saucepan. 'She's a natural. Her husband will be a lucky man.'

Ric felt his aunt's words like a kick in the gut. The thought of Lyssa having a husband one day, some guy back in Australia—there was so much wrong with that picture that for a moment he just stood there, speechless.

But Lyssa laughed off Maria's words and the familiar sweet sound of her laughter swept away the image and brought the smile back to his face. It always had that effect on him.

'Gino's being my taste tester.' She waved a floury hand towards the other side of the table. 'And doing a very good job of it.'

Ric jerked. 'Gino, I didn't see you there. I hope you are well?'

Gino raised a hand in greeting. '*Si, si,* I am very well, *grazie.* And much, much better since I met Lyssa. She is very beautiful, no?'

Ric's eyes flickered back to Lyssa's face and saw her cheeks turn a brighter pink. Because of Gino's words? What had been going on here while he'd been outside with Alberto?

'Yes, she is,' he muttered, moving closer to the table. He didn't like having to agree with Gino as if he was the first one to notice. *He'd* met Lyssa first. He knew how beautiful she was. He did not need it to be pointed out to him.

'We have been having a very good time. We

have been talking. She has been telling me about the tour you have given her, Ricardo, and I have been telling her what I would have done differently. I appreciate what you have done. It was very good of you to take my place as you did.'

Gino held out his hands, palms up, as he shrugged his shoulders. 'You did the best you could. It is such a pity that I had my accident because Lyssa deserved to have the best experience we could give her.'

Ric's head whipped around to glare at Gino. He was older than Ric, mid-thirties at least, but shorter and smaller in build. He supposed Gino would be considered handsome, but he wouldn't look so handsome with a broken nose.

'Pastry,' Lyssa said, her voice bubbly and cutting through his anger.

Or was it jealousy?

'I've never made pastry in my life. When my mum wanted to teach me, I had better things to do with my time. But now…well, sit down and try it for yourself.'

He moved close to her as she reached for a large tart filled with fruit which already had a section cut out of it. 'I made this.'

'It looks very good.'

Her eyes sparkled and her enthusiasm rolled off her like an aura, surrounding him. He couldn't resist brushing at the smudge of tomato on her cheek with his thumb. Her skin was warm. And soft. The softest skin he'd ever felt.

Her eyes looked into his. 'I'm probably covered in mess.' Then she turned away and focused on slicing the tart.

His gaze dropped to her lips, pink and parted in concentration, and the desire to kiss her again nearly turned him inside out. But when he glanced up he met his aunt's gaze. Maria smiled and returned to stirring her pot. He glanced in his uncle's direction. Alberto was busy peering into the fridge and, relieved, Ric let go of the breath he'd been holding.

He didn't want his uncle to feel he'd let him down by becoming over-familiar with Lyssa. His uncle's approval was as important to him as his own advice seemed to be to Alberto.

Lyssa had set a plate and fork in front of an empty chair. 'Aren't you going to try it?' She pointed at the slice of tart she'd cut.

'Yes.' He sat down and ate a forkful. 'It's perfect.'

Lyssa beamed at him then went back to the dough she was working on. He watched her kneading a lump of it with firm but gentle hands and the sensual rhythm mocked him.

He was going crazy.

Deliberately, he lifted his eyes. 'Will you be ready to leave straight after lunch?'

'What?' Lyssa looked at him, then her face fell. 'Oh, I forgot we were leaving today.'

His heart twisted painfully in his chest. He could hardly wait to be alone with her and yet she was disappointed at the thought of leaving here with him. Hadn't she been as moved as him by last night's kiss? He'd been sure she had.

'No, no, no,' Maria said, waving her spoon in the air. 'Stay another night. There is no need to rush off, is there?'

'Well, yes, there is,' Ric said. 'Lyssa wants to spend some time in Rome before flying out. It's where her parents come from.'

'One more night, that's all. It won't make such a difference.'

Ric gave Lyssa a questioning look. 'It's your choice. Do you want to cut short the time you have in Rome to stay here a little longer?'

She chewed on her bottom lip in the way that had become familiar. 'I'd like to spend another night here,' she said after a moment, 'but I'll be very disappointed if I don't see Rome.'

He mentally ticked off the remaining activities. 'We could forget about climbing Vesuvius.'

Maria flapped her free hand. 'You don't want to do that, Lyssa. It's hard work. And the dust and pebbles get in your shoes.' She shook her head. 'It is not worth it.'

Lyssa brightened. 'Actually, I wouldn't mind giving that a miss. So, does it mean we can stay here?'

Ric nodded, resigned to having to wait another twenty-four hours before it would be just the two of them again.

Gino had been listening to the discussion while he finished off his slice of tart. 'In fact, Ricardo,' he said, 'there is no need for you to continue with the tour. Now that I am recovered I can accompany Lyssa for the remainder of her time in the country.'

'*No.*' The word was out before he could stop it and much more forcefully than he would have liked, but he couldn't help it. Spending time with Lyssa was not something he would give up easily. She'd be going home soon. He'd have to accept that. He didn't have to accept Gino's offer.

'No, thank you. I'll continue. It would be unfair to Lyssa to change guides now.'

'Oh, I am sure Lyssa would be very happy to

change, no?' Gino didn't give her a chance to answer before he went on. 'You have done more than enough, Ricardo. We must not inconvenience you any longer than necessary.'

'Lyssa is not an inconvenience,' Ric said firmly. She was a lot of things, but not that.

'No, no, no, I did not mean that she was an inconvenience. My apologies, Lyssa, if you thought I was saying so.'

Lyssa laughed. 'I didn't, Gino.'

'Ricardo has a very important football career. We would not want to risk his recovery by imposing on him.'

Lyssa looked across the table at him, her eyes narrowed. 'Do you need to rest your knee?'

'No.'

'Because I could finish the tour with Gino if it's a problem.'

'It's not a problem. I told you before, my knee is fully recovered.'

'But Lyssa would have the benefit of an experienced tour guide—'

He silenced Gino with a serious glare. 'I will continue with Lyssa.'

'Yes, Ricardo should finish what he has started,' Maria said, turning off the stove and coming back to the table, where she poked a finger into Lyssa's dough and gave her an encouraging smile.

Alberto nodded. 'Thank you for the offer, Gino, but Ricardo will finish the tour.'

Gino sighed dramatically. 'Ah, I see I must give in. I am devastated.' He put a hand on his chest and sighed again. 'Are you sure, Ricardo?'

Oh, Ric was sure. He couldn't imagine *not* spending these last few days with Lyssa. He loved her company.

Love?

Was that where this was heading?

Surely not. They were having fun, that was all. He wasn't stupid enough to fall in love again. He'd tried it once and it had been a disaster.

'Ric?'

Lyssa's voice jolted him back to the present. 'I'm sure. Of course I'm sure.'

But he was distracted now. He needed to be alone to think. He felt as if he was teetering on the edge of a precipice and, if he wasn't careful, he'd fall. But would that be a bad thing?

He definitely needed to think. He made an excuse to escape outside and strode towards the orchard, remembering what an idiot he'd been over Valentina. He'd been so in love with her he'd have done anything, gone anywhere. If it would have made her happy, he'd even have given up football.

He grimaced at the thought. What would his life have been like if he'd done that? *Dio*. Thank God he hadn't. It was football that had saved him when Valentina dumped him. It had hurt. No, that was an understatement. It had nearly destroyed him when he'd discovered she had never felt the same way, that he had been the equivalent of the proverbial notch on the bedpost.

Besides, giving up football would not have impressed Valentina. It was the game that had attracted her to him in the first place.

He'd been naïve then. He hadn't known that there were so many women who wanted nothing more than to sleep with and be seen with a sports star. Once Valentina had gone, there had been plenty more to take her place. They were all beautiful, had great bodies and didn't mean a damn thing to him.

He'd never trusted a woman again. None but his aunt. Nor would he give up football, for *any* woman.

Dropping to the ground, he sat with his back against a lemon tree, the fragrance of its blossoms reminding him of the previous night, of kissing Lyssa. He closed his eyes and leaned his head on the smooth trunk.

Lyssa was just as beautiful as those women in Milan. More so, because hers was a natural beauty which wasn't hidden beneath a sophisticated veneer. Whether she went all out to impress with her hair straightened and her face made up, or whether she left her hair to do its own thing and her face bare, she was the same woman. And just as desirable.

He'd thought Valentina was the pinnacle of beauty, but, now that he'd met Lyssa with her fresh-faced loveliness, Valentina just seemed overdone. Overbleached, overtanned, overstyled. There was nothing natural about her.

But Lyssa was a different type of woman altogether. She wasn't someone he could toss aside like all the others. She could get hurt.

Why hadn't he thought of that before? What had he been thinking when he'd started to flirt with her?

He'd been thinking that she was sweet, caring, funny and positive. That she was honest. That she was the type of woman he could trust. The type of woman he could marry.

Dio.

Now he was in unfamiliar territory.

For so long he'd been determined that he wouldn't get married, would never get so close to a woman that the subject would even raise its head.

But before Valentina had broken his heart, he *did* have hopes and dreams. He *had* wanted a family of his own. A wife—one who would love him the way Maria loved his uncle Alberto. He couldn't have been shown a better example of how love could be.

Children. A home. Stability. With a woman who loved him for himself, not for his career.

Could those dreams come true with Lyssa?

Of course not. She was going back to Australia. To her life there, and his life was here.

Unless he asked her to stay.

He jumped to his feet and paced while his mind turned over the all-important question.

Would she stay if he asked her?

The answer was dependent on whether she felt the same way about him—the same as he felt about her. But how was that exactly? Which brought him back to the question that had sent him running from the kitchen.

Did he love Lyssa?

He stopped pacing and stared at the ground. Did he have to be sure before he could ask her to stay? Or could he ask her to give them a chance to see where this relationship went?

The next day Lyssa wondered whether she could cope with much more morning sickness. How bad did it have to get before it got better?

She'd have to ask the question when she got back to Australia. She'd go and see a doctor as soon as she arrived. In the meantime, she'd have to put up with it and do her best not to let Ric know because she didn't want to spoil their last few days.

She didn't have much time left to enjoy the special relationship she'd discovered with Ric, and sharing the news that she was pregnant would definitely wreck what they had.

When she returned to her room, Maria was waiting there with some plain biscuits on a tray.

They hadn't spoken about her pregnancy, but when Maria held out the tray with a sympathetic look Lyssa burst into tears.

Maria sat next to her on the edge of the bed and put an arm around her shoulders. 'You are having a bad time, no?'

Lyssa nodded. There was no point in denying it. 'I was fine when I left home. It's all started since I've been here.'

'You poor girl. I had a bad time with Marco, my first. Luca was not so bad and Gianni, well…' She snapped her fingers. 'No trouble at all.'

'Well, that's comforting, because I don't think I could stand the thought of going through this a second time.' She shrugged. 'Not that there is any likelihood of a second time.'

Maria hesitated, then said gently, 'I haven't heard you mention a husband.'

'No.' She sighed heavily. 'I'm not married.'

'Are you going to marry the baby's father?'

'No. He's not in the picture any more.'

'He was a bad man?'

'Yes.' Lyssa sniffed and dried her eyes now the tears had stopped. 'Well, yes and no. I mean, we were in a long-term relationship and I thought we would get married and be a family. But I was wrong.'

'He refused to take responsibility?'

'He didn't want children. He didn't want to marry me. He left me when I told him I was pregnant. Now that I know what kind of man he is, I don't want him near me. I made a huge mistake.'

Lyssa dragged up another sigh, then flinched. 'Oh, that sounds terrible. I didn't mean to make it sound like I don't love my baby, because I do.'

She rubbed her belly with her palm. 'I won't ever let her feel like she was a mistake.'

Maria smiled. 'I am sure you won't. You don't miss him? The baby's father?'

'I feel sorry for my baby not having both parents, but I can't do anything about that except love her twice as much. For my sake, no, I don't miss him at all.'

Tilting her head, Maria said, 'There are other fish in the sea, no?'

'Oh, I don't mean that.' Lyssa's cheeks grew hot. 'I'm going to stay single from now on.'

Maria's eyebrows shot up. 'No, no, no, that is not a good idea.'

'I'm perfectly capable of looking after my child on my own.'

'Of course, but you will be lonely.'

Lyssa opened her mouth to argue, then clamped it shut again. She *would* be lonely. As soon as she left Ric, she'd find out what lonely really meant. And she'd spend the rest of her life wondering what it would have been like if circumstances had been different when they met. Very different.

When she made it downstairs, Ric was looking at his watch. He'd said it was important to start early to avoid the crowds at Pompeii and she'd kept him waiting while she wallowed in self-pity upstairs.

'I'm sorry, Ric. Will we be too late now?'

He turned, his frown disappearing as soon as he saw her. She loved that. She loved the way he always looked so pleased to see her.

'We won't have time to visit both Herculaneum and Pompeii, so I suggest we go straight to Pompeii.' He crossed the kitchen to her. 'That's if you're well enough to go at all? You look tired.'

She forced a smile. If she only looked tired, she must look better than she felt, but the nausea was wearing off now and by the time they reached Pompeii she'd be her normal self. 'Of course I'm well enough to go. I'm disappointed about missing Herculaneum but I wouldn't miss Pompeii for anything. You should know that by now.'

He nodded. 'I do.'

She approached Maria, who was working at the kitchen table again. 'Maria, thank you so much for *everything*, and especially for the cooking lessons. I'm so grateful for your time.'

Maria wiped her face with the back of her hand before turning to hug her tightly. Lyssa had to force back her own tears. There was something about this family that enabled every one of them to get under her skin in record time.

'We will see you again,' Maria said, after kissing her on both cheeks. 'I know we will.'

Although Lyssa knew it wouldn't happen, she couldn't help wishing Maria was right. She gave the older woman another hug, then glanced at Ric. He was watching them closely but she couldn't read his expression.

She said a muted goodbye to Alberto. She was feeling too emotional after hugging Maria to say much to him. He expressed his disappointment at her departure, then she followed Ric out to the car.

'You and Aunt Maria have taken a liking to each other, haven't you?' Ric said as they clicked on their seatbelts.

Lyssa sniffed, trying hard to hold back the tears that were stinging her eyes. 'Do you mind if we don't talk about it?' Her voice cracked.

He gave her a concerned glance. 'Of course.' After a long moment, he said, 'I had a phone call this morning while I was waiting for you. It was to see if you approve of the names that the children have chosen for the puppies. I told them you would.'

'What are they?'

'Sydney, Melba and Alice.'

Lyssa gave a burst of laughter. 'Oh, very good. I think they had a bit of help to come up with those names.'

'I'm sure they did. Good choices, aren't they? They will suit them when they are full-grown dogs as much as they suit them as puppies.'

'Brilliant.' She bit her lip as the rogue thought entered her head that she wished she'd see the puppies grow up.

Ric kept the conversation going and she was grateful. By the time they turned off the main road for the *scavi*—the excavations—she'd shaken off the sadness of leaving his family. Or rather, she'd pushed it to the back of her mind, which meant she would have to deal with it later, along with everything else.

Entering old Pompeii through Porta Marina—which Ric explained had been a lot closer to the sea before the eruption—Lyssa's first impression was of oppressive heat. If she'd been able to leave early, as Ric had suggested, they could have avoided the hottest part of the day. Not to mention the hordes of tourists who made the ancient streets seem as crowded as they must have been before the disaster.

There were tour guides all around her, speaking in different languages to their groups of visitors. Most of them seemed to be speaking German or English and she listened for a moment to the guide nearest to her.

His speech sounded fascinating, but she had Ric and he'd be able to tell her more than any of these guides. He was the most knowledgeable guide she'd ever had. And the most interesting man she'd ever met. She slipped her arm through his possessively and he smiled down at her, clearly pleased.

'We might get separated in this crowd,' she explained.

He squeezed her arm into his side. 'I won't let anything happen to you. I promised, remember?'

She smiled back. 'I remember.'

He led her further into the city, where they spent hours exploring the ruins of the markets, the baths, the bakery and the brothels. It was like entering a time machine. She saw wide streets with ruts cut in the paving stones by the wheels of chariots, the entrance to a shop with graffiti on the wall beside it, grand houses with beautifully preserved wall paintings and colonnaded gardens.

Ric did a great job of making the tour fun as well as moving. He started with the less impressive sights—which she found very impressive—and built up to the areas where more and better frescoes had survived.

But the most striking sight was that of the people of Pompeii overwhelmed as they tried to escape the horror that hit their city. After nearly two thousand years, plaster casts made from body-shaped cavities in the hardened ash bore witness to the panic that must have taken place.

Still affected by the sight, she was glad when they sat on a low wall to look at the aqueduct system in the public baths.

'I can just see myself as a Roman coming here after a hot morning in the forum,' she said. Then, 'How did they heat the water?'

'Slaves. Underground, slaves kept fires burning beneath boilers and the hot air passed under the floors of the baths. Simple as that.'

'Hmm. Simple, but they must have been diabolical working conditions for the slaves.' She sighed. 'OK, I've seen enough.'

She jumped up, then immediately wished she hadn't when a wave of dizziness hit her. She felt all the blood drain from her face. She swayed. She reached for Ric but he was too far away, and then everything went black.

* * *

The next thing Lyssa knew she was in Ric's arms, pressed against his solid chest.

She lifted a hand to her forehead. 'What's going on?'

'You're conscious. Thank God.'

'I passed out?'

'You did. You terrified me.' Ric's voice shook and his concern touched her.

'I'm really sorry, but you can put me down now. I'm OK. I can walk.'

'No way. I'm taking you to hospital.'

'But—'

'Don't argue. You hit the ground hard. You might have concussion or something.'

She sucked in a sharp breath. She'd hit the ground hard? Had she hurt the baby?

She couldn't feel any pains in her stomach, which was a good sign, wasn't it?

Or was it? She didn't know.

She clutched a handful of Ric's shirt and turned her face into his chest, becoming aware of the rapid beat of his heart beneath her cheek. He was anxious too but he was only worried about her—and she was fine. He didn't know there was a genuine reason to worry.

At least it meant he would get her to hospital as quickly as he could and she was grateful for that. As for what might happen when they got there, she couldn't think about that now. All she could do was focus on her baby and will her to be all right.

CHAPTER NINE

FROM the other side of the corridor, where he was leaning against the wall, arms folded across his chest, Ric kept his eyes fixed on the door of Lyssa's private hospital room.

How much longer could it take? He'd thought checking for concussion was a fairly simply matter, but he'd been waiting for hours now.

What if there was something seriously wrong? He'd feel terrible if something happened to her. When he'd seen her fall, his heart had nearly stopped. Partly because he'd promised to look after her and had failed, but it was the way *he'd* feel if anything happened to her that had scared him the most.

Holding her in his arms on the way to the car, he'd decided that when she recovered he'd tell her how important she'd become to him. He'd tell her how he felt.

The door of her room had opened from time to time; there'd been plenty of coming and going, but no one had been prepared to tell him what was going on.

Finally the young doctor he'd spoken to when he'd brought Lyssa in emerged, made eye contact and crossed the corridor to him.

'You are Ricardo Rossetti, aren't you? I thought you looked familiar when we spoke earlier but things were a little busy then. I am a big fan.' He gave Ric a broad grin.

Ric frowned, impatient. He wouldn't normally be rude to a fan, but right now all he could think about was Lyssa. 'Doctor, is she all right?'

The doctor's grin vanished and his manner became professional. 'Yes, she is well. She suffered no ill effects from the fall. Neither did the baby.'

Ric's eyes widened. Did he say *baby*?

'It looks like she fainted because she was dehydrated. Morning sickness will do that and apparently she has been having a rough time with it. I have told her she has to keep up her fluid level in future, especially if she is going out in the sun.'

Morning sickness. The reason he never saw her until mid-morning. He'd just accepted that she was a late riser, but this made everything clear—why she often looked pale and tired in the mornings, why she had stopped eating breakfast with him.

'I understand she hasn't seen a doctor in Australia yet.' He gave Ric a questioning look.

Ric shrugged. 'I don't know.'

'Well, she will need to do so when she gets home. We ran some routine blood tests and it looks like everything is fine. Apart from the dehydration, of course. She is on a drip now, but as soon as it's finished she can leave. You can go in to see her now.'

The doctor held out a hand and Ric shook it mechanically, then turned towards Lyssa's room.

Now he had the opportunity to tell her how he felt, to ask her to stay in the country and give their relationship a chance, but he was confused.

She was pregnant and he'd had no idea.

Why hadn't she been truthful?

He'd believed she was honest. He'd thought her the most honest woman he knew. How could he have been wrong about her?

Had she considered her pregnancy a minor detail? Too unimportant to talk about? He shook his head. Such an attitude didn't fit the image of the Lyssa he thought he knew. But he'd thought they were close. Friends at the very least.

A nurse entered Lyssa's room and through the open door he saw her in the bed, propped up on pillows, staring out of the window. When she looked round and spotted him her eyes lit up and she broke into a smile, but almost as quickly the smile became hesitant and her eyes wary.

The nurse let go of the door and, before it closed in his face, he reached out to catch it. He felt he had no choice but to enter the room and, once inside, he stood on one side of the bed while the nurse fiddled with the drip on the other side. Satisfied at last, she smiled at both of them, then left.

'How are you feeling?' he asked after an awkward silence.

'Fine, thank you. I was just dehydrated.'

'Yes, the doctor said so. He also said it was because of morning sickness.'

She dropped her gaze and her fingers pleated the white sheet. 'Yes.'

He cleared his throat. 'You're pregnant, Lyssa? It's true?'

She nodded.

'Why didn't you tell me?'

She dropped her head against the pillows

and closed her eyes. Her face was still pale but not the stark white it had turned just before she'd collapsed.

He pushed a hand through his hair. Between the fear he'd felt then and the shock from hearing she was pregnant, he couldn't think straight. He'd just been getting used to the idea that he might be in love with her and that the idea didn't scare him, when he'd had the fright of his life and thought he'd lost her. Then she'd come round and he'd experienced the greatest sense of relief he'd ever known, only to be hit between the eyes by this news.

Was it any wonder he didn't know how he felt about it?

'Because…' Her voice broke and she coughed before trying again. 'Because there was no need for you to know.'

He walked away from the bed, raked at his hair again, then swung back. 'Didn't you think I had a right to know once we'd kissed? Didn't that change things?'

Her eyes open wide now, she shook her head. 'No. It was…only a bit of fun…wasn't it?'

He froze, pinned to the spot. So much for believing she might feel the same way about him. He had the answer to his question now.

He unclenched his jaw and forced himself to speak normally. 'Yes, of course. You're right.'

She looked down at her hands.

'Who is the father?'

'My ex-boyfriend.'

In a flash of memory, he remembered her saying she hadn't had a boyfriend for a while. It couldn't have been very long. He closed his eyes at a sudden stab of pain between his shoulder blades. Bringing himself under control, he lifted his chin. He had to act as though this were unimportant. He couldn't let her see how shaken he was. She'd laugh at him.

Perhaps not. She wasn't Valentina. She was still the soft-hearted Lyssa he'd fallen for. The only difference was that she was pregnant with another man's baby.

Dio. He was such an idiot. As Lyssa had said, their relationship was supposed to be fun and nothing more. That was how he'd approached it, and clearly she'd done the same. But whereas he'd made the mistake of wanting something more, something deeper, she hadn't. He could hardly blame her for that and it wouldn't be fair on her now to let her see what a fool he'd been.

'Right.' He made an effort to sound in control, of both himself and the situation. 'The doctor said you can leave as soon as the drip's done its job.' He nodded at the clear plastic bag of fluid hanging at her side. 'Looks like it's about halfway through, so I don't suppose it will take long to finish. I'd better go and arrange a hotel for us.'

She nodded again.

'Then tomorrow, if you feel up to it, we'll drive on to Rome and do some sightseeing before you fly home.'

She lifted her head then and her expression shook him. She looked so unhappy. He couldn't understand why. As far as he could see, she had nothing to be unhappy about. But even so, the sadness in her moist eyes made his chest ache. He wanted to take her in his arms and tell her everything would be all right.

But would it?

'Who will look after you when you get home?'

'I don't need anyone to look after me.' She paused. 'But there's my family. They'll make sure I'm OK. Once they get over the shock.'

'They don't know?'

She shook her head.

'But the baby's father knows?'

'Oh, yes. That's why he's my *ex*-boyfriend.' Her words twisted his gut. He wanted to grab the man by the throat for doing this to her. For his own sake as well as hers. But he didn't have the right, nor would he have the opportunity.

'I'm sorry, Lyssa.'

'Don't be sorry. I'm glad he's gone. I'll… we'll be fine on our own.' She patted her stomach gently.

Keeping his voice level, he said, 'I'll be back in an hour or so,' and headed for the door.

As soon as he made it to the privacy of his car, he thumped the steering wheel with both fists. He'd been so close to falling in love with Lyssa. So close to telling her how he felt. To asking her to stay.

It was lucky he'd learned the *minor detail* of her pregnancy before he'd made a complete fool of himself the way he had over Valentina. But he didn't feel lucky. He felt as though every time he allowed himself to love someone, they left him.

Why hadn't she told him about the baby? She must have had a reason for keeping quiet. They'd shared so many of their thoughts during the hours they'd spent together. Surely, such important information would be at the forefront of her mind?

Perhaps she simply thought it was none of his business, that a passing holiday fling had no need to know such an intimate detail.

His gut tightened again at the thought that he meant nothing to her. That while he'd been falling for her, she'd seen him only as a short-term romantic interest, not as a serious contender for a relationship.

But maybe it was for the best. If she'd shared his feelings then things could have become much more complicated now that her pregnancy was part of the equation. His life wasn't an ideal one for children. He couldn't imagine Lyssa wanting to raise a child in the celebrity-filled world he inhabited, and he had no plans to leave it.

The thought of Lyssa with a baby brought to mind a very different world. But he couldn't think about that now. It wasn't his baby she was having. He had no place in her life. She would leave soon, would go back to her family, and he would return to his career.

Lyssa waited for the door to close behind Ric before letting the tears fall. She'd had her work cut out to hold them in once they'd filled her eyes. But she'd been determined not to break down in front of him. She didn't want him to know how deeply she'd fallen for him. She had no intention of embarrassing him like that.

Nor herself for that matter.

She'd known all along that everything would change between them if he discovered she was pregnant. That was why she'd been unable to tell him.

Well, she'd been right. She'd seen it in his eyes as soon as he'd spoken. All the warmth and teasing humour had left them, to be replaced by politeness—as if she were someone he'd met in the street. No one special.

They'd come full circle. From now on he'd be escorting her out of duty to his uncle. Nothing more.

If only she hadn't fainted, she wouldn't have ruined her last few days.

The end result would have been no different—she'd still have had to go home to reality—but if the truth hadn't come out, she would have had a few more precious days with Ric—to be held by him, kissed by him, to create more memories. And, as pathetic as she knew it was, she would have treasured those extra memories.

Well, she'd have to make do with those she had.

She'd still be with Ric between now and catching her flight, but it wouldn't be the same. She would have to pretend that she didn't care deeply for him. She would have to act unconcerned about leaving.

It would be hell. She didn't know how she'd get through it.

She had to remember, though, that she did have something to be thankful for: her fall hadn't hurt the baby at all. And if Ric finding out about her condition was the price she'd had to pay for that good news, then she couldn't complain, could she?

Even if her pregnancy hadn't changed things, nothing could have come of their relationship. Even if by some miracle he had still wanted her when he found out about the baby, she would never have fitted into his world. More importantly, she could never have brought a baby into that world.

The next day, Lyssa and Ric arrived in Rome. She was just as awed by being there as she had been the first time. Despite everything else she'd thought about her life having changed since she was last there, the way she felt about her father's birthplace remained unchanged.

They checked into the same hotel as Lyssa had used on her previous brief stay and entering Reception brought back memories of seeing

Ric for the first time, leaning on his Lamborghini, looking unbelievably gorgeous and utterly bored.

Back then, she'd thought her heart was safe from him because she was strong enough to resist. How wrong she'd been.

As she unpacked, she realised that the next time she used her suitcase it would be to leave for the airport. The time when she'd have to leave Ric was very near.

And as if that was not enough, it meant she'd soon have to tell her mum and dad that she was going to have a child but not a husband. She hoped she'd be able to make them see that she could do this, that being a single parent wouldn't be so bad.

It wouldn't be easy, but she'd do it. Her parents would help her once they got over the shock. Her brothers would help too. Between them they'd make up to the baby for the lack of a father.

She wouldn't even dream about one day finding a man she could marry. She couldn't imagine finding another man like Ric, and if she couldn't have the real thing she'd rather be alone forever.

She shook herself, refusing to give in to

sadness again. She'd cried enough tears. She only had a short time left with Ric and she was *not* going to spend it moping. She didn't want his last memory of her to be of a watery-eyed grump. If she could do nothing else, she could do this. She could leave him with a cheerful memory.

She'd do the best impression she could of someone who was happy. And she *was* happy to be in Rome—if the circumstances had been different, she'd have been on top of the world. So, if she acted as if she were enjoying herself, she might start to believe it.

After meeting him downstairs for lunch, Lyssa went with Ric to a *trattoria* and had the speciality, deep-fried courgette flowers. It was a wonderful meal, but for once she didn't care about the food. She made an effort to eat anyway. She knew it was important for the baby.

After lunch Ric suggested a stroll to the Forum, the centre of ancient Roman political life, and, once there, Lyssa was completely captivated by the place. They wandered the fields of ruins, gazing up at the tall columns of temples. She could almost hear the chariots and the *Hail, Caesars*.

Leaving the Forum, they passed a statue of

the She-Wolf, the creature that according to legend had brought up Romulus and Remus. It made Lyssa think of the puppies.

'I wonder how Sydney, Melba and Alice are getting on,' she said.

Ric had been quiet. Not giving her the silent treatment exactly, but not sharing his knowledge as freely as normal, not explaining every little historical detail, which was something she'd grown used to during the trip. Today he'd given her the facts but no more.

She missed the *more*.

She missed his voice. She missed his touch, his lips. She felt empty without them. But she kept the stupid smile plastered on her face. He mustn't know how dumb she'd been.

'I could make a call to find out,' he said, a smile tugging at his lips for the first time since she'd seen him enter her hospital room.

'That would be great.'

She waited while he made his call and watched him, imprinting the image on her mind to recall later—as if she could forget—but for some inexplicable reason it seemed important to remember every detail of this moment. The exact expression on his face, his tone as he spoke

Italian to his cousin's wife, the way the sun high-lighted one section of his blue-black hair.

He flipped his phone closed, startling her, catching her staring.

'Apparently all three dogs have settled in and Sydney's causing havoc. Nina says he's chewed up a pair of Ferragamo satin shoes.'

'I don't know what that means exactly, but it sounds bad.'

'Marco has promised her two pairs if she'll let Sydney stay.'

She winced. 'He's safe?'

He nodded, smiling. 'He's safe. Melba and Alice are paragons of virtue in contrast.'

'It will be nice for them to be able to meet up when their families get together. I didn't thank you for arranging that.'

He shrugged off her words. 'No need.'

'Well, thank you anyway.'

The Colosseum was breathtaking but when Lyssa saw the queue to go inside she lost all her enthusiasm for it. She turned to Ric. 'I think I'd like to go back to the hotel.'

He gave her a searching look. 'Are you feeling dizzy again? Are you going to faint?'

'No, nothing like that, but I think I've done enough for this afternoon.'

'Then you're probably right.'

He took hold of her elbow and his touch just about turned her to jelly. It was the first contact between them since she'd passed out at Pompeii and she'd thought that would be the last.

She was only a little tired but she let Ric support her as they descended a flight of steps which opened onto a *piazza*. Lyssa gasped at the striking picture made by a bride in a simple and elegant wedding dress, apparently having her album photos taken.

She looked so happy and so beautiful. When the groom joined her for the next shot and she gazed lovingly into his eyes, Lyssa tried to suppress her envy but couldn't stop a sense of loss from bubbling over. She would never experience this for herself, would never wear a gorgeous wedding dress, would never—and this was the blow that hurt the most—would never marry the man of her dreams.

'It's wedding season,' Ric said flatly.

Only then Lyssa realised that everywhere she looked in the *piazza* there were brides, in every style of dress from minimalist chic to something resembling a carnival float.

'Now, that's overkill,' she muttered. 'I got it the first time. No need to rub it in.'

'What was that?'

She shook her head at Ric's puzzled frown. 'Nothing. I'm being silly.'

They made their way back to the hotel via a maze of small streets, dodging Vespas in the narrow passageways.

'You should sleep before dinner,' Ric said when they reached the hotel foyer. 'Would you like to eat in your room?'

'No.' She smiled. 'I appreciate your concern but I'm fine. I will sleep but I don't want to miss dinner.'

He nodded. 'I'll ring you. I'll give you plenty of time to wake up.'

Ric watched Lyssa go and felt something contract inside him. She looked pale. It was unlike her to cut short their sightseeing. Was she feeling ill and hiding it from him the way she'd hidden the morning sickness?

It made him feel sick to his own stomach to realise she'd suffered and he hadn't known anything about it. He wished she'd told him, then he would have been able to take better care of her.

She was carrying another man's baby, true, but she was still Lyssa. For some reason she'd kept things from him, but she was still the same person. And as much as he tried, he couldn't like her any less.

Walking the streets of Rome with her today had made him realise how empty his life would be once she'd gone. It had already lost a lot of its appeal now that he couldn't take her in his arms and feel her soft curves pressed against him.

The thought of going back to Milano didn't thrill him either. His old life didn't attract him the way it used to.

He had to admit it surprised him that Lyssa didn't feel more than friendship for him. He could have sworn there was real feeling behind those kisses they'd shared. So much that he found it hard to believe she could put their stalled relationship behind her so quickly, but clearly she had.

It had been nothing more than a holiday flirtation for her. That was why her smile had barely faltered today. There had even been a few occasions when her eyes had seemed distant, as if she was already thinking about going home. And that had nearly killed him.

That evening they dined at a terrace table looking out over the dome of the Pantheon and were served by a team of elderly waiters whose greetings were pure Italian charm. They were a joy to watch at their work. With much bowing and ceremony, they made an event of every dish.

Lyssa could hardly contain her amusement when her salad was swished through the air and presented to her as if it were the rarest delicacy. Ric's risotto was given the same royal treatment and, when the waiter moved away, she burst out laughing.

'I'm sorry,' she said behind her hand. 'I tried not to laugh but…'

Ric's eyes twinkled with amusement. 'I don't think he heard you.' He glanced at the waiter's stooped back as he disappeared inside the restaurant. 'I don't think he can hear much at all, but we'll know if we don't receive our next course.'

She laughed again, feeling more relaxed with Ric than she had in a couple of days, and reached for her glass to take a sip of water.

Ric watched as she lowered the glass. 'Is your pregnancy the reason you don't drink wine or coffee?'

She nodded. 'I don't drink wine because there are conflicting studies about how much alcohol is safe and I prefer to be sure I'm doing the right thing. And I went right off coffee straight away.

I still like the smell of it but I can't drink it.' She picked up her fork and began to eat.

She saw his jaw clench for a moment before he said, 'I wish you'd told me.'

'Why? It doesn't make a difference, does it?' She'd meant that she didn't drink wine and coffee, but as soon as the words were out she realised it sounded like something else altogether. 'I mean—'

'No, I suppose it's not important at all,' he said tightly. 'It's not as if there was ever going to be anything serious between us.'

The lettuce was suddenly as hard to swallow as a giant fishbone. 'No. It's not.'

They lapsed into silence. After several long moments, Lyssa sighed. 'I've been thinking.'

'Yes?'

'The tour is over. Once you brought me back to Rome you were officially off the hook. There's really no need for you to stay on.'

Something flashed in his eyes. Hurt?

'Do you want me to leave?'

She stared. 'That's not what I want.' If only she could tell him what she really wanted. 'I'm just saying that I'll understand if you want to go. It's not as if you're under any obligation to stay and I'm sure you have other things to do.'

'Well, I think I am under an obligation. Until I see you safely on that plane, I will feel responsible for you.'

She bristled. 'No one is responsible for me but me. And I'm perfectly capable of looking after myself, you know. I have travelled extensively, and mostly on my own. I've appreciated having your help on this tour, but I would have survived if I'd done it alone.'

Holding up his palms, he said, 'Sorry. Responsible is the wrong word. I didn't mean to imply that you couldn't look after yourself. I just need to see you board that flight in one piece, to be sure you're safe.'

She softened. It was impossible to stay angry with Ric. Impossible for her anyway, especially when his protective nature was one of the things she found endearing about him.

'After you've seen me on board, you won't have any idea what's happening to me,' she said.

'No.' His face was impassive before he turned away to watch the entire elderly team of waiters gather to ceremoniously deliver a fish to a neighbouring table.

She wanted to ask him if he'd care, but pride stopped her. Pride and the fact that she knew the answer. She'd been a passing interest but one he'd forget about as soon as she'd gone. And any lingering memory would be obliterated as soon as he returned to his life and the women in Milan. Women with whom she had no hope of competing. She wasn't even in the same league.

'Have you made your decision yet?' she asked.

Ric took a moment to steel himself before looking back at Lyssa. She was wearing the dress she'd surprised him with that first night but her curves seemed more pronounced. She must have gained a little weight during the time he'd known her. It suited her, made her appear even more feminine and beautiful. Made it even more difficult not to blurt out that he wanted her to stay. That he hated the thought of not knowing what was happening to her on the other side of the world. Hated the idea of never seeing her again.

He even hated the thought of never seeing her with her baby, and that confused him. He knew she would be a great mother and it bothered him that he would never see her in that role.

He wished it was his baby she was carrying. He wanted her to be the mother of *his* children.

She'd asked him a question and he didn't need to ask what decision she was referring to. It was, after all, the single most important decision of his adult life. Or it had been, until recently. He hadn't been able to give it any thought of late. All thoughts had been shunted from his brain by Lyssa.

'Not yet,' he said at last. 'I'm still thinking.'

She nodded. 'Well, good luck with it. I'm sure the solution will fall into place when you're least expecting it.'

'Are you?'

'That's the way these things usually happen, isn't it? We can think and think and think about a question, but it's when we stop thinking that the answer comes to us. Our subconscious minds seem to know more about what we want than we do—than our conscious selves, that is.'

He shrugged. He could only hope his subconscious could work out the mess that was in his head because he certainly couldn't.

He mentally put all sensitive subjects aside for another day and, making a deliberate effort to sound cheerful, asked, 'So, what do you think of Rome now that you've finally seen it?'

'I love it, of course, as I always knew I would. I feel connected here.' For a moment, she narrowed her eyes in thought. 'I was thinking today that a lot of Rome's charm comes from the fact that so many people live in apartments above where we were walking, in those places in the narrow alleyways with the little Juliet balconies.

'I know there are loads of tourists in the city too, but it's the communities living and working in the city that make it magical.'

He loved to hear her talk like this. Her enthusiasm for whatever subject she was discussing warmed him right through. He crushed an urge to ask why she didn't move here if she liked it so much. He knew why. Her life was on the other side of the world.

'I thought it was the history you liked best?'

'That too. Especially the mix of the two.' She waved her hands across each other. 'It's the mix that makes Rome so special.'

But what was it that made her so special that his gut reaction to her presence seemed to intensify every time he saw her?

He was acquainted with women a hundred times more sophisticated, but it wasn't sophistication that did it for him. It was the dancing light in her eyes when she talked, her humour and her soft heart. Her courage, her smile, her empathy.

He gritted his teeth. Only one more day and then he'd have to say goodbye to her, wish her well in her future life, and act as though he didn't care. He did care, but he had to let her go.

'Only one more day,' he repeated out loud.

Her face fell. 'Yes. That's right.'

'So we'd better make it a good one.'

She gave him a wobbly smile. 'What do you suggest?'

CHAPTER TEN

LYSSA knew how she'd like to spend her last full day in Italy.

In Ric's arms. Making the most of every second.

But nothing like that was on the agenda. Instead they strolled to Piazza Navona, once a stadium that held chariot races and now a place for people-watching.

Lined with Baroque *palazzi*, it had three fountains including a masterpiece by Bernini in the centre, and was full of artists drawing on-the-spot portraits of tourists. For a moment Lyssa was tempted to ask Ric to sit for one, but thought better of it. He'd question why she wanted it and she wouldn't be able to hide how much he meant to her.

The atmosphere buzzed with tourists, locals, teenage schoolkids, business-people and women shopping for dinner, all moving around the *piazza* as if they'd been choreographed.

They sat at a café table, trading comments on the *piazza*'s sights and characters while sipping on iced water and munching mid-morning pastries. Then they set off to join other tourists stopping at the Spanish Steps, gazing at the Trevi Fountain, wandering along the wide Via del Corso.

In Via Condotti, Rome's finest shopping street, Lyssa gazed dumbfounded at the windows of all the famous designers—and some designer names that even she had heard of—then she spotted the store of Salvatore Ferragamo.

'Oh, look at the price of those,' she said, pointing at a pair of leopard-print shoes. 'Do you think the ones Sydney chewed cost as much as that?'

'I expect so,' Ric said.

Appalled, she turned from the window. 'Now I feel terrible.'

'It's not your fault. And don't forget Marco's going to buy Nina some replacement shoes.'

'Two pairs!'

She could pay the rent on her little apartment for months for the cost of two pairs of those shoes—well, maybe not months, but weeks—

and very soon she'd be in the position of trying to find that rent on her own.

No. She must not get sucked in by negative thoughts. This was her last day with Ric. Her last full day. He was going to drive her to the airport the next morning, but that didn't count because then she wouldn't be able to ignore her imminent departure. Today she didn't have to think about it, and she wouldn't. She planned to live in the moment.

After a quick lunch back at the hotel, they climbed into Ric's car and he drove out to Hadrian's Villa, which immediately became another highlight of Lyssa's trip. She was simply awed to stand on the sprawling property where the Roman emperor had spent his time off from building walls across Britain and other such projects.

They walked around the ruins while Ric explained the network of hidden tunnels through which Hadrian's slaves had brought him food while he relaxed in the spa area. Apparently, Hadrian hadn't wanted to see his slaves.

As Ric talked she didn't just hear his voice, she felt it. Her insides seemed to vibrate in time with his words. She stopped walking and stood for a moment, her eyes closed, listening and feeling.

Then she felt something else: his arm around her waist.

Her eyes flew open and he was standing there, looking down into her face.

'We'd better go,' he said. 'The heat. It's getting to you, isn't it? Have you been taking enough fluids? Here, drink some water.' He handed her the bottle he'd been carrying.

She took the bottle and drank deeply before she spoke. 'I'm fine. I'm not going to pass out. At least, I don't think I am.'

In spite of her words, she leaned against him a little. It would be so easy to lean fully into his strength. To pretend she was ill. To let him take care of her. If she was lucky he might even carry her again.

'Your eyes were closed. I thought you were going to fall down.'

She swallowed. He was concerned. It would only take a few words and he'd scoop her up into his arms and carry her to the car. She'd be able to enjoy the experience this time because she wouldn't be worried about the baby.

But that would mean lying to him and she couldn't bring herself to do that. Not deliberately. Not again. Sighing, she capped the water bottle and handed it back to him, then moved forward, away from the tempting tingly warmth of his arm.

'I promise, I'm not going to faint,' she said over her shoulder.

He caught up with her. 'Still, if you've seen enough here, I know somewhere we can go to cool off.'

She flicked a glance his way. His expression told her there was no hidden meaning behind his words. He wasn't suggesting a skinny-dip in Hadrian's beautiful reflecting pool.

Of course he wasn't. He wasn't interested in her that way any more.

'Sure,' she said, suppressing a sigh. 'Let's go.'

A short drive away they came to the town of Tivoli, and soon after entered the fountain-filled gardens of the Villa d'Este.

After the heat of Hadrian's Villa, it was like stepping into an alfresco shower. Everywhere she looked Lyssa saw water, gushing from fountains, cascading over small waterfalls, trickling from rock features and spurting from sculptures.

The gardens were on different levels and, after climbing enough steps to last her a lifetime, Lyssa sat on a wall, where she welcomed the fine mist of water that landed on her.

'This was a good idea,' she said. 'You were right about it being cooling.'

Ric sat next to her and immediately she felt the awareness that always gripped her when he was near. She was going to miss him so much. She wondered how he'd react if she reached for him now, pressed her lips to his. Would he kiss her? Or would he push her away?

Not that it mattered. She wasn't going to try it. Because she wanted more than kisses. Much more. She wanted the love that for such a short time she'd seen in front of her like a mirage. Then it had vanished, taking with it the life she'd briefly dared to dream about.

And who was to blame? Certainly not Ric. He'd never made any promises. He'd never led her to expect anything from him. The dream had been all her own doing.

But she believed that things happened for a reason. There had to be some purpose to her having met Ric and she was pretty sure it was meant to be a lesson for her. A lesson in what she wanted from life. From love.

She'd learned that she wanted to be loved completely and unreservedly, and if she couldn't have that she wouldn't settle for less. From anyone. Even from Ric, the man of her

dreams—if he offered her the type of relationship she assumed he had with the woman in the
magazine, she'd turn that down too.

In future, it was all or nothing for her.

The drive to the airport the next day seemed a
lot shorter than the forty-five minutes Lyssa
knew it took. Time seemed to be in a rush. From
the moment she'd woken up, she'd had to hurry
to keep up with the clock, all the time knowing
this was the day she'd fly away from Ric, that
it was only a matter of hours before she'd have
to say goodbye. And she wasn't ready.

Checking in took no time at all and then she
joined Ric, who was studying the departures
screen.

He turned as she reached his side. 'All done?
No problem?'

She nodded, her throat too tight to speak.
She'd barely managed to answer the questions
at the check-in desk.

He jerked his head at the screen. 'It's on time.'

'Good.' A delay would have been better. Just
a short one, like, maybe, a lifetime.

But this was pointless. Wishing things could
be different was a waste of energy and she had
limited stocks as it was. Plus, any more time she

spent with Ric now was just prolonging the agony of parting.

'Let's go to the departure gate.' He indicated the direction they needed to take.

She drew a deep breath. 'You don't have to come with me, Ric. There's no need for both of us to wait.'

For an instant his expression changed and she thought she saw a glimpse of pain as raw as her own. But then it was gone and she shook off the illusion. *She* was the one who'd been stupid enough to fall in love. *She* was the one who was suffering here.

'Let's go,' he said again and this time she just nodded.

Before long they were sitting side by side at the departure gate, staring straight ahead. In silence.

It wasn't the companionable silence she'd come to know well with all the time they'd spent in the car together, sitting quietly during gaps in conversation.

This silence was full of palpable tension.

After a while, Ric cleared his throat. 'It's been nice to know you, Lyssa.' He made a frustrated gesture. 'Not *nice*. That's not the right word.'

Suddenly his accent seemed thicker, more Italian.

'Special. It has been very special to know you.'

Lyssa sucked her lip between her teeth and bit it hard. When she felt she had the tears under restraint, she finally spoke. 'It's been really special knowing you too, Ric.'

She hoped her voice didn't sound as wobbly as her stomach felt. She gave a small cough. 'Ric, I want to thank you. You've been a terrific help—'

'No, I do not want your thanks.'

'But—'

'Lyssa,' he said quickly, then drew a deep breath, 'Lyssa, I hope you have a good life. A happy one.'

She tried to moisten her lips. 'Thank you. You too. Whatever you decide to do.'

He nodded.

Sighing, she said, 'I wish things had been different.'

Ric twisted towards her. 'How?'

She picked at the fabric of the fixed seat, considering her answer. She couldn't say she wished she hadn't been pregnant when she met him. That would be like saying she wished her child didn't exist and she never wanted her to hear her mother say something like that.

Nor could she say she wished Ric were different, because she loved him just as he was. How could she say she wished he weren't a footballer, when he'd made it clear how much that meant to him? It was the most important part of his life.

It was impossible to answer his question. They just weren't meant to be together. No matter how much that hurt, it was true.

She gave him a helpless shrug. 'I don't know.'

He searched her face for a moment, then straightened in the seat and they lapsed into silence again.

'Your parents won't be happy to hear your news, will they?' he said after a while.

She gave a short crack of laughter. 'That's an understatement. They're going to be very disappointed in me, but they'll have to get used to it. I'm going to show them that I don't need a husband.'

'Why did the baby's father leave you?'

'Because he doesn't want children. He doesn't want the responsibility of them.'

She hoped Ric didn't think that was a dig at him, but she couldn't help it. He'd asked.

Ric looked as if he was going to say something else but he was prevented by the announcement that her flight was boarding.

'*Dio.*'

She stood up, swinging her handbag onto her shoulder. He stood too, facing her. For a second he looked unsure, as if this was as difficult for him as it was for her. Then he reached for her hands.

She kept them clenched at her sides. She couldn't let him touch her or she'd fall apart, and she'd done so well up to this point.

He stepped closer and took her fists into his palms, stroking his thumbs across her knuckles. She had to close her eyes and will herself not to react to his touch. This would be the last time she'd feel his strong hands.

Ever.

At that thought she opened her fists and threaded her fingers into his, her stomach nearly turning itself inside out.

Their eyes locked. His dark eyes seemed to see right past the defensive wall she'd tried to erect. It crumbled under the power of his gaze. He let go of her hands and pulled her into his arms. She knew a moment of confused hope, but then the public-address system brought her back to reality with the final call for her flight.

She pulled back.

He cupped her face in his hands. 'Be careful, *cara.*'

'I will.' With those words she turned from him and hurried through the boarding gate.

By the time she reached the plane, tears were already leaking from her eyes no matter how hard she tried to hold them in. She managed a shaky smile for the flight attendants as she boarded then, after strapping herself into her window seat, she pressed the heels of her hands against her eyes and gave way to silent sobs.

Ric shoved his hands in his pockets and rocked back. She'd gone. She'd left. And if he'd thought Valentina had broken his heart, he'd just learned that her betrayal had been a mere scratch. It was nothing to having his heart ripped out and taken to the other side of the world.

The sense of loss was more like the death of his parents.

He sat heavily.

He'd wanted to kiss her one last time. But he hadn't had the guts. What if she'd pulled away from him?

He missed her so much already that he ached. Ironic, he thought bitterly, that for the first time in years he'd wanted a relationship with a woman that went beyond the physical, and the fact that he couldn't have her caused a physical pain.

He tried to imagine going back to the life he knew, the life he'd thought he couldn't give up, and found it no longer appealed. The game, the training, the parties, the women—all the emphasis was on the physical side. With Lyssa he'd been involved on an emotional level and he didn't know how he could return to anything else.

He'd always liked the fast pace of his life, but perhaps it hid the fact that there was something missing from it. He definitely didn't miss the constant activity, the excitement. But he did already miss the peace he'd felt in Lyssa's company.

Loneliness wrapped around him like a thick fog. When he went back to Milano he'd have his teammates, his girlfriends, but would they prevent him feeling lonely? A few weeks ago, he'd have said yes.

He looked up at the throngs of people milling around the airport. He'd never felt more alone. He needed to talk to someone, and he knew where he had to go…where he always went when he needed reassurance that he was loved. The thought hit him between the eyes. He had to see his uncle and aunt. He had to go…home.

* * *

Walking into Maria's kitchen brought back memories of seeing Lyssa there and his heart twisted painfully in his chest. Memories of feeling jealous when she smiled at Gino. He could even smell the fruit tart she'd made.

His uncle, seated at the table, looked up. Maria was at the sink, washing vegetables. She turned as he closed the door behind him, and froze, searching his face. 'Lyssa…?'

He leaned against the door. 'Gone.'

Maria dropped a potato into the sink. Water splashed everywhere but she didn't seem to notice. She hurried towards him. 'Ah, Ricardo. I'm so sorry.'

He returned her hug, just for a moment allowing himself to draw strength from the familiar affection. Then he eased back, looking down into her face. 'What are you sorry about?'

She frowned. 'You did ask Lyssa to stay, didn't you?'

He shook his head.

Maria hit his shoulder. 'Idiot.'

The shock made him step away from her. His aunt had never raised a hand to him since he'd come to live with her at twelve years old.

'Why not?'

He tried to gather his thoughts. Why hadn't he asked Lyssa to stay? 'She's pregnant.'

'Yes, yes, I know. But why didn't you ask her to stay? You love her, don't you?'

He pulled out a chair and sat opposite his uncle. 'I do, but how did you know?'

Maria sat next to him. 'Ricardo, I am getting old but I am not stupid.' She nodded. 'At least, I thought you were close to admitting it to yourself. Lyssa, on the other hand, I had no doubt about.'

His mouth dried. 'What?'

'No doubt at all.' Maria sighed. 'She reminds me of myself as a young woman. Anybody could see she is in love with you. Did you at least tell her how you feel?'

He shook his head.

Alberto held up his palms. 'Please. Slow down. Maria, what are you saying?'

She gave him an incredulous look. 'What do you think I am saying? That Ricardo is an idiot to let Lyssa go back to Australia without telling her that he loves her. Argh!' She threw up her hands. '*Men.*'

'It's not that simple,' Ric said. 'She's…' He glanced from his aunt to his uncle and then stared at his hands splayed on the table. 'She's having another man's baby.'

'I know.'

He rubbed his forehead. 'Did she tell you she was pregnant?'

'No. I am a mother and a grandmother.' Maria looked at him as if that explained everything.

'I wish I'd known. I might have been able to look after her better. She collapsed. At Pompeii. I took her to hospital in Napoli.'

Maria inhaled sharply. 'Is she all right? The baby?'

'Both are fine. It was dehydration.'

After murmuring a prayer of thanks, Maria pinned him with a serious look. 'So, what are you going to do now?'

What he wanted to do was spend the rest of his life with Lyssa. He wanted to take care of her. But, of course, things were not so simple. He shrugged. 'I don't know.'

'You want to bring her back?'

He nodded. 'But I can't ask her to share my life in Milano. It wouldn't be right for her, especially not with a baby.' And that wasn't what he wanted anyway. He wanted to create a real home with Lyssa.

'No, of course not. But you could bring her here,' Maria said, her eyes lighting up at the prospect. 'To your home.'

Ric swallowed. 'I could retire from the club. It's what they want.'

'Well, if you want something to do, you can take over the tour business. Let your uncle rest.'

Ric eyed his uncle. 'But you want to pass it on to one of your sons, don't you?'

Alberto reached for Ric's hand, grasping it tightly. 'Don't you know, Ricardo, that we regard you as one of our sons? Have we ever treated you differently, or given you any reason to feel less important to us than Marco, Gianni or Luca?'

Ric returned the pressure of his uncle's hand, and in that moment something cracked inside him. 'No. You haven't.'

'We love you, Ricardo. We have since the day you came to us, a sad, broken little boy. But you never wanted us to tell you so. I think you didn't want us to take the place of your parents.'

He heard Maria sniff and, when he looked her way, saw tears streaming down her face. His own face felt wet too. 'I was scared. I was frightened that you would die too.'

For the first time in sixteen years, Ric accepted that he'd always held his uncle and aunt at arm's length. Because he'd believed that if he admitted that he loved them, he would lose them.

But he did love them and they'd stood by him all this time. They'd loved him like a son.

He was silent for a long moment, thinking. He loved Lyssa and there was no reason why he shouldn't love her baby too. Just as his uncle and aunt had loved him. They'd taught him it was possible.

He could have a family with Lyssa and her baby, and perhaps further children, and now that he'd let himself think about it he knew it was what he wanted.

'There is something you should consider, though,' Alberto said gently. 'Lyssa might not want to live here. She might prefer to stay in Australia. Her parents are there.'

Ric didn't hesitate. 'Then I will stay in Australia with her.' He would find something to do; he had enough money to set himself up in whatever business he chose. Now that he knew what he wanted, the rest wasn't important. As long as he was with her, he would have everything he needed.

'Do you really think that Lyssa loves me?' he asked Maria. Warmth filled him at the thought. 'You think it's possible after such a short time?'

A low laugh came from Alberto. 'Entirely possible. Ricardo, forty years ago your aunt and I had only one weekend together and then I had to go away. Luckily, she agreed to marry me before I left.' He lifted Maria's hand from the table and kissed it. 'I am glad I recognised our love for what it was. Something very special. When you find the one for you, love is just there. No amount of time can alter it.'

Ric watched his uncle and aunt exchange loving smiles. One day he wanted to tell their children and grandchildren how he and Lyssa had met and fallen in love. He wanted to share a private smile with her in forty years' time. He wanted what Alberto and Maria had, and he wanted it with Lyssa. No one else.

But did she want it too?

Lyssa had been home for twenty-four hours when she finally felt able to face the world. Well, not the world exactly, just Chloe.

When Chloe opened the door, her expression told Lyssa that she hadn't done as good a job with her make-up as she'd thought.

'Lord, Lyssa, what's happened? Is it the baby?'

Lyssa shook her head, a protective hand going automatically to her stomach. 'She's fine.'

'Well, come in, sit down and I'll make a cup of herbal tea. Peppermint OK?'

'Yes, but do you have time? If you're busy…'

'Sit. You're going nowhere.'

Lyssa sat.

While Chloe made the tea she looked around the apartment that was a mirror image of her own. Chloe had gone to town with colour and it worked surprisingly well in the small space. Now that the apartment next door was all hers, she could do whatever she liked with the place—within reason, of course, since it was a rental, but she could decorate it to match the bright colours of the platter she'd bought in Vietri sul Mare.

Remembering that day brought back memories of Ric, and the tears she'd thought under control welled up again.

The strong aroma of peppermint hit her nostrils before Chloe appeared with two mugs and placed them on the low table between the matching red sofas.

'Here.' Chloe grabbed a box of tissues from a side-table and pushed them across to Lyssa. 'Now, tell me what's going on.'

'Nothing.' Lyssa blew her nose. 'Not now, anyway.'

'Is this about Steve? Because if you're crying over that loser, I swear I'll—'

She managed a laugh. 'I don't care about Steve. Good grief, he's ancient history.'

'That's what I thought. So…?'

'I met someone else.'

'In Italy?'

She nodded.

Chloe let out a low whistle. 'You were so determined not to even look at another man while you were there.'

'Yes, well, it was difficult not to look at Ric.'

'Bit of a hunk, was he?'

She recalled his face, his physique, his sparkling dark eyes, but most of all his smile, and sighed. 'You could say that.'

But then there was also his voice, his teasing and his protectiveness. She loved and missed everything about him, not just the physical side. She had to take a deep breath to control the sadness that rushed in.

Nodding, Chloe lifted her mug and settled back on the sofa. 'Tell me all about him.'

So Lyssa did. Starting with how she'd thought he was an insensitive, superficial playboy, and finishing with falling in love with the man underneath the good-looking surface.

Chloe stared at her for a long moment after she stopped talking, then said, 'He sounds gorgeous. Why did you come home?'

Lyssa wiped a hand across her forehead. 'Oh, Chlo, everything changed after Pompeii.' She told her friend about her impromptu trip to hospital.

'Hmm. He dumped you because you were sick?'

'No, no, it wasn't like that at all. I knew he wouldn't be interested in a pregnant woman and I knew he never had anything serious in mind. I was just a convenient distraction for a while.'

Chloe pulled a face. 'Lord, you can pick them, can't you?'

She hadn't *picked* Ric. She'd had no choice in the matter. What she'd felt for him had just been there, whether she wanted it or not.

'I'll never forget him, Chlo. I'll never stop loving him either. He's the guy I'll measure every other man by. But he's not here. It's just me and bub.'

She pressed a hand against her stomach again. She had no right to indulge in self-pity when she had a child to protect. 'Now I have to concentrate on having a healthy baby and bringing her up the best way I can. Alone.'

'Her?'

Lyssa smiled. 'I think so.'

Chloe grinned. 'I can't wait. But hang on, what about telling your parents?'

'Tomorrow. There's a family lunch.'

'Will you be OK?'

She thought about it for a moment. 'Yes. I'm not looking forward to it, but it has to be done.'

CHAPTER ELEVEN

LYSSA sat in her little car outside the house where she'd grown up. With its pillars and stone lions, it proudly proclaimed itself the home of an Italian-Australian family, like most of the houses in the suburb.

She was in no rush to go inside.

Her brothers' cars were already parked in the front driveway. She was the last to arrive for the family lunch.

Sighing, she told herself not to be a wimp. She was an adult, about to be a parent herself. She could do this.

Yeah, sure, like she'd been able to tell them she was moving out of the family home. What an uproar it had caused when they'd learned that Steve was also moving into the apartment she'd signed up for. Now she was going to tell them that their worst predictions had come true.

But she was not the same person she'd been back then. She'd been through a heck of a lot in recent times. First the pregnancy test, then the showdown with Steve, the realisation that she would be raising her child alone, and finally the trip during which she'd met the man of her dreams, and lost him.

Leaving Ric behind without a fuss had taken all her strength, but also made her a stronger person. It was as if she'd lived through her worst nightmare and survived. The ordeal had changed her and she would never be the same again.

Her parents, however, were still the same old-fashioned people. She knew how much she was going to upset them and that was what was stopping her. She dreaded seeing the hurt and disappointment in their faces.

But facing her parents with courage was all part of proving she was capable of bringing up a child on her own. She had to show them that she was no vulnerable young woman in need of protection, but a strong, independent mother-to-be.

She flung open the car door. It wouldn't get any easier no matter how long she sat outside, so she got out of the car then steeled herself to enter the house.

Everything seemed the same as normal in the Belperio family. Lyssa was the only one who knew that everything had changed. Her brothers teased and goaded her as they always had, her father sat in his favourite chair and reminisced with her about the Rome he knew in his youth while she told him about the sights she'd seen. Her mother fussed over the meal, dashing between the kitchen and the large table, and complained about Lyssa being late.

'You're only just in time,' she said to Lyssa. 'What kept you? You're not working too hard, are you?'

'No, Mamma. I'm not working too hard.' She followed her mother into the kitchen and picked up the salad bowl she found waiting on the side-bench. 'Actually, I have some news.'

'Good news?'

She swallowed. 'I think so, yes.'

'What is it, another job? Where are you going this time?' Her mother flapped a hand as she spoke. 'No, wait till we're all sitting down. Tell us all at once. Don't spoil the surprise.'

She bustled off again and Lyssa looked down at her hands clenching the rim of the bowl. Making an effort to relax her grip, she carried the bowl to the table and set it down.

Within minutes, her mother had finished fussing and had ushered the family to the table. When all five of them were seated, she said, 'Now, Lyssa has some news so be quiet for one minute and let's hear what she wants to tell us.'

Lyssa looked at the expectant faces, then took a deep breath.

'Don't tell us you're going to get a proper job,' Dominic said. 'One that involves working for a living?' He burst out laughing as if he'd told a great joke.

She pulled a face at him.

'Was that a car in the driveway?' Her mother jumped up and rushed to the window. 'Yes, it is. Who could this be, visiting now when we're just about to eat?'

Lyssa dropped her head into her hands. This was hopeless. She couldn't blurt it out before the visitors came in; she might as well have broken the news in a phone call.

'Are you all right, *carina*?'

She raised her head at the note of concern in her father's voice. 'Yes, Pappa. I'm fine, really.'

The door from the front hallway opened and her mother popped her head around it. 'Lyssa, it's someone for you.'

'Me?' Her eyes widened when a grinning Chloe leaned past her mother.

'Chlo? What are you doing here?' Pushing back her chair, she went around the table to meet her friend.

Chloe's grin stretched even wider. 'I've brought you something.'

'What?' When she reached the door she looked between the two women. 'Ric!'

Her stomach lurched. This was surreal. Even in her dreams, she'd never imagined seeing him here, in Australia, in her parents' house. 'I don't…' She shook her head.

'I'm sorry to interrupt lunch.'

Oh, she'd missed his voice.

'Lyssa,' Tony grabbed her arm and her attention, 'is that Ricardo Rossetti, the soccer player? It is, isn't it?'

She nodded.

'What's he doing here?'

'Well…' She looked back at Ric and words eluded her. She lifted her hands and dropped them in a bewildered gesture. 'I don't know.'

Ric's eyes were on hers and she couldn't tear her gaze away. The look in his eyes—she'd missed that too.

'May I talk to you?'

She nodded.

Chloe said, 'You know, I'm starving. Do you mind if I eat your lunch?'

'No—'

'There's plenty,' Mrs Belperio told Chloe. 'I will get some for you.'

Lyssa watched her mother hurry off to the kitchen. Chloe followed, giving Lyssa a wink as she passed by.

Lyssa stepped into the hallway and closed the door behind her so that she was alone with Ric. She took a moment to breathe in, to convince herself that she wasn't hallucinating. She could see, hear and smell him.

'How did you find me?'

He flicked his hand. 'No problem at all. You gave me your address to arrange shipment of the platter that you bought. Remember?'

'Yes.'

'And Chloe saw me knocking at your door. She…interrogated me.'

For a moment she thought Ric had struggled to find the right English word, then realised he was spot-on. Chloe would have interrogated him. The fact that she'd brought him here to Lyssa's parents' house must mean she approved. She would never have done the same for Steve.

'Shall we go outside?' she asked as a burst of voices reached them through the door. She heard Tony saying Ric's name repeatedly.

Ric held out his hand and she placed hers in it without hesitation. Oh, she'd missed that too, the sensation of his warm hand surrounding hers, sharing his strength.

She'd missed him.

Her heart pounding, she went through the front door with him and across the front lawn to sit at the edge of the fountain. She was about to ask him whether he remembered the last time they'd sat at the edge of a fountain, but she kept quiet. For now, nothing was more important than finding out what Ric was doing there.

'I never thought I'd see you again,' she said.

'Did you want to?'

She looked into his eyes. He wasn't teasing. It was a serious question and it deserved a serious answer. She nodded. 'Very much.'

'I wanted to see you again, and if you'll let me I want to see you every day for the rest of my life.'

'What?' The word came out on a gasp.

'I mean it, Lyssa, *bella*. I was stupid to let you go, but I thought…'

His thumb moved across the back of her

hand, adding to the swirling mass of sensations she was already struggling with.

'I hope you'll forgive me.'

'For what?'

'I thought that your pregnancy was the end of everything.'

She shook her head. 'There's nothing to forgive. I understand.'

His other hand lifted to touch her cheek. 'I was going to ask you to stay. I wanted you to be mine.'

A tiny moan escaped her throat. 'But you don't believe in relationships.'

'I didn't, before you.'

'You were really going to ask me to stay?'

Nodding, he said, 'Then I learned you were pregnant and believed that I could never accept another man's baby. I thought it meant there was no hope for us.'

She placed a protective hand on her belly.

'I was wrong. I want you, Lyssa, but I also want a family with you.'

'You said you didn't want children.'

'I know.' He shrugged. 'I think I had been telling myself that for so long that I had started to believe it, but it wasn't true.'

She allowed herself to picture it for a

moment. Ric, herself, children... But then, with a heavy sigh, she pulled her hand away.

'I'm sorry, Ric, but if you're working your way around to asking me to marry you...well, I have to stop you right there.'

His arms dropped to his sides. 'I want to take care of you and the baby.'

'I appreciate that. I do. It's very kind of you to have come all this way, but we don't need anyone to take care of us. We will manage just fine on our own.'

'Kind? No. What are you saying, Lyssa? You don't want to marry me?'

She looked at her hands for a long moment. 'No, Ric. For some reason, you feel responsible for me, but you don't need to. No, thank you, I won't marry you.'

He got to his feet. 'This has nothing to do with feeling responsible for you. I don't. I want to take care of you, yes, but I know you don't need me to do it. I know you can look after yourself. I want to marry you because I love you, not because I feel responsible for you.'

Lyssa gasped. Her head was spinning as she tried to make sense of what was happening. She looked up at him and forced herself to say, 'I still can't marry you.'

'You don't love me?'

'I didn't say that.' She rubbed her temples. 'It's not so simple. I don't fit into your world. I'm not the right type of woman for you and I don't want to be. I can't change to suit your life in Milan.'

'No, no, I don't want you to change. I don't want you to come to Milano.'

Puzzled, she frowned up at him. 'What?'

'I have given up football.'

'But you love it!'

'I love you more.'

Silenced, she stared at him, searching his eyes and finding the truth. 'You love me.'

She hadn't framed it as a question, but he nodded. 'I do. I resigned from the club before I flew out here, and I don't care where we live. I don't want to live anywhere without you.'

'Oh, Ric. You do love me.'

He reached for her and pulled her up into his arms. 'Please say you love me a little too.'

His lips were so close and she touched hers to them. 'I love you a lot, Ric. I think I loved you the moment I saw you leaning on that yellow car.'

He broke into a smile. 'Was it the car that you fell in love with?'

'No, I don't think so,' she said, laughing.

'Good, because I'm going to sell it and buy a minibus.'

'You are? Why?'

'For all the children we're going to have.' He gathered her closer and kissed her, claiming her lips with a firmness and certainty that calmed any lingering doubts.

'You haven't said you'll marry me,' he reminded her when he finally stopped kissing her.

'No, well, I'm a bit worried about all these kids you say we're going to have. How many are you talking about?'

He shrugged. 'Five, six. How many do you want?'

'I haven't really thought past one.'

'This one?' He touched her stomach tentatively. 'I'm going to love this baby as if it were my own.'

'She, not it.'

He gave her a questioning look. 'She?'

'I think so.'

He grinned. 'I swear she will never feel as if I love her any less than I love all her brothers and sisters.'

She nodded. 'But let's keep an open mind about the number and see how we go, shall we?'

'Whatever you want. I don't care how many.

But I meant what I said about loving her. My uncle and aunt love my sisters and me as much as they love their own children.'

'Of course they do.' With a contented sigh she said, 'I'm so glad you realise that now.'

'I think I always did but couldn't admit it.'

She was quiet for a moment, pensive. 'Are you sure you won't miss your old life? It's been so important to you for so long.'

'If I didn't have you, I would miss it. To be honest, though, I was becoming a little tired of all the parties and so on.'

He tried to tuck her hair into its clip but there was too much of it. She reached up and pulled out the clip so her hair tumbled over her shoulders.

'That's better.' He smiled. 'It's beautiful.' Looking into her eyes, he said, 'Travelling with you, passing the time doing nothing but enjoying your company and our surroundings, it reminded me that life doesn't have to be fast, or loud, or expensive to be good. We had a good time, didn't we?'

She nodded. 'We sure did.'

'That's what I want from now on.'

'I want it too,' she said softly.

'You are going to be a wonderful mother. I

wouldn't want anyone else to be the mother of my children.'

'I wouldn't want anyone else to be the father of mine.'

Their eyes locked.

'Have you told your parents about this baby yet?'

'No, not yet. I was just about to do so when you turned up.' She ran her hands up his arms and linked her fingers behind his neck. 'I still have to do it.'

'But you don't have to do it alone. She's going to be my daughter too.' He threaded his fingers into her hair, then tipped back her head to kiss her again.

'Your lunch is getting cold.'

They sprang apart at the sound of Lyssa's mother calling from the front door.

Lyssa touched Ric's jaw. 'Can this wait till later?'

'Are you going to marry me?'

'Yes, of course.'

'Then it can wait. We have the rest of our lives.'

'Come and meet my family? They're going to be yours too.' She turned towards the house.

'We can buy a house near to them if you want to.'

'You'd really live here?'

'I told you, I don't care where I live as long as it's with you.'

She hugged him. 'My parents came to Australia to give their children a better quality of life than they had, but they were quite poor, so coming here gave them a chance to improve their circumstances.

'I think it has always been my own destiny to go back to Italy. I used to feel it when my father talked about his birthplace. And when I was there, I felt I belonged.'

'Are you saying you'd like to live there?'

She nodded. 'I think so. We could try it for a while, couldn't we? Maybe we could live with Maria and Alberto.'

'There is nothing I would like more,' he said, smiling. 'I'd like to help Alberto with his business, perhaps take it over.'

'Really?' She gave him a surprised look.

'Yes, we talked about it before I came over here.'

'Well, that's great. It sounds like a good idea to me.'

'I think it was your idea.'

'Just remember that next time I have a good idea.'

'Your mother is still waiting.' He took her hand.

Not just waiting, but nearly bursting to know what was going on, Lyssa thought as they walked towards her.

'Like I said, Mamma, I have some news. Come on, I'll tell you when we're all sitting down.'

EPILOGUE

LYSSA picked her way carefully across the debris-strewn ground to join her husband watching construction progress.

Ric turned and spotted her. 'Careful, *cara*.' He hurried towards her and supported her over the last stretch.

She pushed a hand into her aching back. She'd be glad when the baby was born. 'It's going well, isn't it?' She waved her other hand in the direction of the project.

After mumbling a complaint about builders in general, Ric agreed that it was coming along nicely.

'And it's going to look just like the walled garden at the Lunettas' farm. At least, it will when the plants have grown.'

'Let us finish building the apartments before you start putting in plants.' He shook his head at her in mock exasperation, but a smile threatened to spoil the effect.

'Oh, you'll have time. I'm going to be busy for a little while.' She stroked her belly. 'But it would be good to have it looking nice before the next tourist season.'

'It will be ready, don't worry.'

She nodded, happy that she'd convinced Ric to expand the accommodation for guests. Not that he'd needed much convincing. Building a pair of guest apartments in a walled garden meant the house could be reserved for family— for their children, for Alberto and Maria, and for other family members who came to stay from time to time.

It was a cheerful family home. Once Ric had allowed himself to love and be loved, it had been natural for him to take the place of a son to Alberto and Maria, and become much more involved with their lives. It was a place he could have had all along if he'd only dared.

With Maria's help, Lyssa was learning to cook well enough to cater for overnight guests and she loved hosting tourists from other countries. She enjoyed chatting to them and never had time to get lonely when Ric was away taking care of business.

Ric's sisters had just come to stay for a while, Chloe was already on her way from Australia and her parents would arrive any day now. They were looking forward to seeing their first grandchild.

They'd been upset when they'd heard about her pregnancy, as she'd known they would be, but having Ric around had helped to lessen their disappointment. It hadn't taken them long to see that Ric was totally devoted to her and the baby she was carrying—just as devoted as if she were his own daughter. And they'd been overjoyed when, a little while later, she and Ric had announced their intention to marry.

It still made her smile to think of their version of a *small* wedding, but then, Italian families just didn't do small weddings. At least it had been arranged in record time so that she could return to Italy while she was still able to travel.

Ric had approached Steve about adopting the baby and she didn't expect him to raise any objections. He'd made it very clear how he felt when he walked away from her. But whether the adoption went ahead or not, theirs would be a real family and she couldn't be happier.

She grinned up at her fantasy man—only

hers, all hers. 'Your daughter's practising her goal-kicking.'

'Oh, really.' He placed a hand on her huge bump and grinned back at her. 'No daughter of mine is going to play football.'

She thumped his arm. 'She'll do whatever she wants to do.'

'Even travel the world alone?'

'Except that.'

Laughing, he slid his arms around her. 'A very clever person once told me that you have to let young women have their freedom. It's the twenty-first century, after all.'

'Yes, but there are limits.'

'But—'

'Shh.' She kissed him.

'I like your way of ending an argument,' he said. 'I might have to start lots of arguments.'

She pushed a hand into her back again. 'I think this baby might be here before my parents arrive.'

'Really? What makes you say—?'

She grasped his arm and held on tightly till the contraction passed. Then she laughed at the comical expression of concern on his face.

'I just know, OK?'

With his arm around her, she started carefully towards the house.

'You will be all right,' he said. 'I won't let anything happen to you.'

She laughed again. 'I don't think you have any say in it this time, Ric.'

Christmas is a special time for family...

...and two handsome single fathers are looking for wives!

The Christmas Baby by Eve Gaddy

Comfort and Joy by Amy Frazier

Available 21st November 2008

A meeting under the mistletoe

Amy's gift-wrapped cop...
Merry's holiday surprise...
The true **Joy** of the season...

For these three special women,
Christmas will bring unexpected gifts!

Available 5th December 2008

www.millsandboon.co.uk

To marry a sheikh!

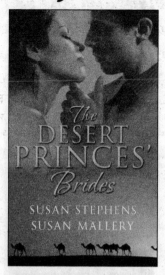

The Sheikh's Captive Bride by Susan Stephens

After one passionate night, Lucy is now the mother of
Sheikh Kahlil's son and Kahlil insists that Lucy must
marry him. She can't deny her desire to share his bed
again, but marriage should be forever.

The Sheikh & the Princess Bride by Susan Mallery

Even though beautiful flight instructor Billie Van Horn
was better than Prince Jefri of Bahania in the air,
he'd bet his fortune that he was her perfect match
in the bedroom!

Available 19th December 2008

M&B

Celebrate 100 years of pure reading pleasure with Mills & Boon®

To mark our centenary, each month we're publishing a special 100th Birthday Edition. These celebratory editions are packed with extra features and include a FREE bonus story.

Plus, you have the chance to enter a fabulous monthly prize draw. See 100th Birthday Edition books for details.

Now that's worth celebrating!

September 2008
Crazy about her Spanish Boss by Rebecca Winters
Includes FREE bonus story
Rafael's Convenient Proposal

November 2008
**The Rancher's Christmas Baby
by Cathy Gillen Thacker**
Includes FREE bonus story *Baby's First Christmas*

December 2008
One Magical Christmas by Carol Marinelli
Includes FREE bonus story *Emergency at Bayside*

Look for Mills & Boon® 100th Birthday Editions at your favourite bookseller or visit
www.millsandboon.co.uk

FREE!

4 Books
and a surprise gift!

We would like to take this opportunity to thank you for reading this Mills & Boon® book by offering you the chance to take FOUR more specially selected titles from the Romance series absolutely FREE! We're also making this offer to introduce you to the benefits of the Mills & Boon® Book Club™—

★ **FREE home delivery**
★ **FREE gifts and competitions**
★ **FREE monthly Newsletter**
★ **Exclusive Mills & Boon Book Club offers**
★ **Books available before they're in the shops**

Accepting these FREE books and gift places you under no obligation to buy, you may cancel at any time, even after receiving your free shipment. Simply complete your details below and return the entire page to the address below. You don't even need a stamp!

YES! Please send me 4 free Romance books and a surprise gift. I understand that unless you hear from me, I will receive 6 superb new titles every month for just £2.99 each, postage and packing free. I am under no obligation to purchase any books and may cancel my subscription at any time. The free books and gift will be mine to keep in any case.

N8ZEF

Ms/Mrs/Miss/Mr .... Initials ....

Surname ....

BLOCK CAPITALS PLEASE

Address ....

....

.... Postcode ....

Send this whole page to:
UK: FREEPOST CN81, Croydon, CR9 3WZ